I0838388

# RESCUED in the ROCKIES

PAT LOCKRIDGE

INK START MEDIA
5710 W Gate City Blvd Ste K #284
Greensboro, NC 27407

Danny's drawing of Little Red

# Contents

# Foreword

*"Through many dangers, toils and snares, we have already come. It is Grace that brought us safe thus far, and Grace will lead us home."* (<u>Amazing Grace</u>, John Newton, 1772)

*"For in him all things were created: things in heaven, and on earth, visible and invisible, whether thrones or powers or rulers or authorities; all things have been created through him and for him. He is before all things, and in him all things hold together."* (Colossians 1:16,17)

We can learn much can about God by observing His Creation. We can observe His love of beauty and the amazing variety of His Creation. We can discover His favorite colors and see His reliance on order in the laws of nature. In this book, Tyler and Danny have the opportunity to observe Creation in the beautiful mountains of Colorado. They learn much about the faithfulness of God as Danny experiences answers to prayer that keep the boys safe. Tyler, a skeptic, has many opportunities to see his views on nature challenged. He struggles with his brother's faith and nature's revelation of Intelligent Design. Will it be enough to turn this troubled boy from his hatred and unbelief?

*"But the basic reality of God is plain enough. Open your eyes and there it is! By taking a long and thoughtful look at what God has created, people have always been able to see what their eyes as such can't see: eternal power for instance, and the mystery of His divine being. So no one has a good excuse [for being an unbeliever]."*
Romans 1:20, The Message

# Prologue

## *A Mother's Prayer*

May 26th

Marianne moaned and rolled over on her cot. She stayed at her work site because of the shortage of space at the hospitals. Her breath came in short spurts, her body ached. She had been unable to keep any food down for two days. Some people recovered. Would she be one of them?

"Dear God," she prayed. "You know that my son, Danny, needs me. He and Tyler cannot survive on their own. Perhaps they are both sick now too. I love you, Lord, and I am eager to be with you in Heaven, but I have responsibilities here. If I do go to be with You, please take care of my boy, Danny, and take care of Tyler too. You know how angry Tyler is because You know everything. Give Tyler faith like Danny has. Help Tyler to know and love you. Thank you, Lord!"

# Super Virus



*You will not fear the terror of night or the arrow that flies by day, or the pestilence that stalks in the darkness, or the plague that destroys at midday.* (Psalm 91:5,6)

Danny (age nine) picked up his phone. It was his friend Alex. "Mom says I can't come to play on Friday. Our schools are closing tomorrow. They've canceled everything. There is a super virus that is making people very sick. It is very contagious too. My mom knows two people who have already died, and now she won't let me play with anyone!"

Danny hung his head as he reported to Tyler (age fourteen). "No school tomorrow or for the rest of the month in Denver! Alex says our schools will be next. He says his mom won't let him come over to play on Friday."

He always looked forward to his play dates on Fridays with his friend, Alex. Maybe his mom could still work something out. His phone jingled again.

"Mom just sent me a text. She says she can't come home tonight. Her building has been put under quarantine. She says to warm up the pizza from the fridge. What does 'quarantine' mean?" Tyler didn't answer immediately. He was playing a game.

Danny grabbed Tyler's phone. "What's quarantine mean?" He asked again with a voice that demanded attention.

Tyler sat up straight. "Huh? What's that again? Maybe it has something to do with a sickness. I heard some people were getting sick in Denver." He began a search on his phone. "Sickness in Denver."

Within seconds several articles came up: "The Super Virus is on a rampage in Denver as it is in many other places in this country. A few isolated cases have now grown to thousands, resulting in an overcrowding of hospitals and hundreds of deaths. The public health department decided that people in areas where more than ten percent of the population is infected should be quarantined. That means no one comes into the area and no one leaves. Family members should seek to return home before the area of their employment receives the quarantine."

Tyler looked concerned. "Marianne says she is not coming home tonight. This is serious. The quarantine lasts two weeks. We won't see her for two weeks. Who will cook our meals and…?"

Danny interrupted: "What if she gets sick? Then what?"

Danny began to cry. "First Alex, then mom? Is this stupid sickness going to make everyone we love stay away from us?"

Tyler shook his head. "Dad is in Afghanistan. His tour of duty isn't over until October, but surely someone will notify him and tell him to come home and look after us."

Tyler hated everything about his situation. He hated that his mom had died of cancer. How could this have happened? Didn't the powers that be know how much he needed his mom? Then he hated his dad for marrying Danny's mom last year. How could his dad think anyone could replace his mom? Marianne had tried to be nice but that only irritated him further. He just wanted to be left alone. Tyler hated that his dad was stationed in Afghanistan, and he had not seen him for months.

Tyler also hated his school. He was upset when he had to change schools and lose his friends as a result of the marriage. Those kids in his new school were always trying to show off, to excel, to be better than anyone else. Tyler had not been good at academics or sports. He couldn't draw, but he did like music. Most of all Tyler hated babysitting his nine-year-old stepbrother, Danny. Danny was outgoing and loved to talk. He always needed attention while Tyler, a "gamer," preferred to be alone. Tyler considered Danny a bother instead of a brother.

Tyler switched on the TV. The evening news was on. "Denver has quarantined most of its neighborhoods and all downtown businesses. Some of the suburban towns, including Aurora and Englewood, have also issued quarantines." The map showed the areas of most cases, fewer cases, and no diagnosed cases.

"Look," said Danny, "Conifer is right next to Littleton, which is going to shut down tomorrow! (He pointed to their little foothills town on the map.) We are going to be next. We will be stuck right here in this house like prisoners. Then we will probably get sick and die like everybody else. We got to get out of here!"

Tyler didn't answer immediately. He was processing. "Stuck here with Danny? Could anything be worse?" He got yesterday's pizza out of the refrigerator and microwaved a couple of pieces. He shoved one toward Danny. "Maybe your mom can get out in a couple of weeks. Let's see what happens."

His phone interrupted them. Tyler read the message in silence. "Looks like our schools are closing a week early. We will have no school tomorrow. At any rate, you better charge up your phone. We won't have anything to do tomorrow except play games on our devices."

The sound of a siren broke the silence as they focused on eating the last of the pizza. Glancing out a window, they caught a glimpse of an ambulance as it passed by on their street.

"See, people are already getting sick in our town." exclaimed Danny. "I say, we got to get out of here. If you won't come, I will go without you!"

The last thing that Tyler wanted was to go anywhere with Danny.

# The Preparation

May 27th

*He will call on me, and I will answer him; I will be
with him in trouble, I will deliver him and honor him.*
(Psalm 91:15)

I t had been two days since Danny and Tyler had felt safe to venture
out-of-doors. They had exhausted all the cold cereal and milk from
the fridge. They were going to have to go to the store soon. Was
Conifer going to be quarantined? If that happened, they could be forced
to stay in their home for weeks. Danny glanced at his cell phone. It was
a message from his mom. "Am not feeling up to par today. Lots of folks
are sick in this building. Guess it will be a while before I can get to you.
Lots of extra cash in second drawer of the nightstand in my bedroom.
God bless you!"

Tyler looked at the message on Danny's phone. "We are going to
have to fend for ourselves. We better find that cash and get some food."

Danny had dissolved in tears. "When am I going to see my mommy
again. I just want my mommy. You don't even care about her, Tyler! I've
got to get to my mommy. God, help me see my mommy."

Tyler was already on his way to the bedroom. He found the cash.
"We better spend this slowly," he said as he counted out nearly a thousand
dollars. This has to last several months. I am going to run to the corner
store. I will go the back way to avoid anyone on the street. I will check

out the situation before entering the store. I don't want to get caught and quarantined today."

"Wait!" wailed Danny. "Don't leave me. I want to come too."

Tyler ignored the plea until Danny grabbed his shirt and hung on tight.

"Ok," agreed Tyler, "but stop your sniffling, and don't make a sound."

The boys snuck out to the alley, then ran from bush to bush. When they arrived at the store, Tyler motioned for Danny to be quiet and stay hidden in the shrubs. He walked cautiously toward the store. Danny hid behind the corner of the building and listened to two customers talking.

"The store is getting low on some things. We had better stock up. It looks like the quarantine is coming to Conifer next, maybe tomorrow or the next day. My family and I are going to our vacation cabin in the mountains. There will be no quarantine there, and we will be free to come and go, catch fish from the stream, and shoot rabbits." "I saw a man come out of the store sneezing. I'll bet he spread his germs around in the store. Now we are all exposed!"

Tyler rushed inside the store, then tried to walk very tall and look older than he was. He bought lots of food that needed no refrigeration including jerky, dried fruit, and breakfast bars. Then he rushed outside to rejoin Danny.

Danny passed the bad news on to Tyler. Tyler took out his hand sanitizer and liberally washed his hands, face, and all exposed skin. "I think those men were right. We will be safer if we go up in the mountains. My dad left lots of great camping gear. Let's get it out and go."

The boys spent the rest of the day assembling their gear and filling two backpacks. There wasn't room for much in the way of clothes, but Tyler wisely insisted that they each take three changes of clothes, jeans instead of shorts and warm hoodies and winter jackets for the cold mountain nights.

The two boys had finished their preparation. "We'll leave in the morning as soon as it gets a little light. We will sneak out the back way. No one will see us, and we can hide in the forest as soon as we are out of town."

Danny's phone buzzed. "This is a notification to the owner of this phone. "Your next of kin has contracted the Super Virus and is being quarantined. You have been exposed and will need to stay at the Celebration Event Center, where all exposed children with infected parents will receive care. Officials in an ambulance will come soon to pick you up."

Danny let out a yelp. Tyler took the phone, read the message and turned out the lights. He knew that if the officials came for Danny, Tyler would be stuck with him in the event center with lots of other kids who might be sick, and they would both face the risk of contracting the virus. He pulled Danny roughly toward the back door. Just then, they heard a knock at the front door. Flashlights were shinning in the window.

The boys, carrying their backpacks and gear, crept out of the back door and walked quickly across their back yard. They passed the gate, and headed down the alley toward the hills. Just seconds behind them, the officials came around the house with their flashlights and a searchlight. Tyler pushed Danny, silent tears streaming down his face, into a ditch. They lay there quietly while the officials searched. They would be safe there for the time being. If the searchers brought dogs, they would be in big trouble.

The people of Conifer were not confined to their homes yet. Most were out doing their last-minute shopping. The noise of traffic and the lights of the cars on the nearby highway distracted the boys and gave them a feeling of familiarity and comfort as they spent their first evening away from their beds. The boys pulled out their jackets and used some clothes to form a make-shift pillow for each of them. Soon the excitement and trials of the day gave way to exhaustion, and they fell asleep.

# The Adventure Begins



*If you will make the Most High your dwelling…then no harm will befall you, no disaster will come near your tent.* (Psalm 91:9,10)

At first light, Tyler gave Danny a jab in the ribs. "Time to get moving. Listen to all that commotion down below." He stood up and peeked through the trees. "Looks like they are still searching for folks, and they have quarantined our town. Look at the patrol car parked in the middle of the road leading to town. It looks like we had better get moving but stay low. They are still looking for us. We should head for that grove of trees."

After about an hour and a half, Danny exclaimed, "Whew, what a climb! I have to rest." He walked over to a fence and leaned against it. A small, red horse (a sorrel) neighed a welcome as she pressed her head over the fence. Danny began to pat her soft, velvety nose. He laughed when her stiff chin whiskers tickled the palm of his hand. He pulled out an apple from his pack—one of the last from his mom's kitchen. The small red horse took the offering. Then two others, a huge black horse, and a buckskin approached the fence. They were also looking for a treat.

"Come on, Tyler. Give them your apple."

"And what are we going to eat if we give the horses our food?" Tyler asked.

Danny seemed not to hear. He followed the little red horse as she trotted up to the small home and outbuildings located off the main road. She walked into the stable. Danny climbed over the fence to be with her. Throwing his arms around the horse seemed to comfort him in his loss.

Inside the stable, an older gent was rearranging some gear. He saw the sorrel sticking her muzzle into Danny's face. "That horse seems to like you," he commented.

Danny responded with enthusiasm, "Oh, I like her so much. I wish I could adopt her."

The older gent introduced himself as Bob Campbell. "I am the caretaker for the Wilsons. They flew to New Zealand a few days ago and left the horses in my care. Where are your parents, boys?"

Danny spoke up, "My brother and I are all alone. My mother is sick and quarantined in Denver. Tyler's dad is in Afghanistan. We want to leave this area before we get stuck in the quarantine.

Tyler looked disgusted and added, "We are not brothers. We are stepbrothers. My dad married your mom, unfortunately! Yes, we are trying to get away so that we do not end up inside the event center with a bunch of sick kids. We have some money.

Bob looked from one boy to the other. "Ever ride a horse?" he asked.

"Oh yes," Tyler replied. "My dad had a ranch in southern Colorado. We sold it to live here with Danny's mom. It has been a few years since I have been on a horse though." Tyler was mentally checking out the buckskin horse. "Just my size," he thought.

"How about you, young fella?" The old gent looked at Danny.

"No, I have only been on the carousel horses, but I would love to ride. I want to buy this little red horse," Danny replied.

"Well, let's see how you do." He snapped lead ropes into the halters on the little sorrel and the buckskin and led them into the stable. "Do you know how to saddle a horse?" he asked Tyler.

Tyler grabbed the saddle blanket and threw it across the buckskin's back.

"This one's Buck, and we call this sorrel, Little Red." He began saddling the little, red mare.

By this time Tyler had the buckskin saddled and was ready to mount. Bob instructed Danny in the proper way to mount a horse. Then the boys took off at a slow walk circling the corral several times.

"Hmmm!" the old gent remarked. "You do pretty well. As I said, I am the caretaker for the ranch and the horses. The only problem is that the Super Virus is moving into this area. I just learned that hospitals in this area cannot handle more cases. The danger of spreading the infection to other patients is great. If I get sick, I want to be close to my family in Florida."

He snapped a lead rope into the halter of the large black horse. As I mentioned, the Wilsons, who own these horses, left for New Zealand. Once they found out about the Super Virus, they decided not to come back right away. These horses only have enough pasture to last a few weeks. If you borrow these animals, they will keep you safe in the mountains. They will also keep you away from the virus and the people who want to put you under quarantine. However, you have to take good care of the animals or you will lose your protection and transportation. You will also need Mr. B. He is a packhorse and will be great for you.

Bob was now moving toward the stable and a pile of supplies. "I can help you pack up. All the tack is here in the stable. I will put the Wilson's contact information in this little metal box. I will throw in a couple of lighters for your campfires as well. It looks like I may be able to get to Florida after all. We have no quarantine to prevent travel yet."

"We also have a dog named Wolf. He is big enough to be a small horse. I do not know if he will be around to go with you. He is really good at catching rabbits."

# Horses!



*Then thundered the horses' hooves--galloping, galloping
go his mighty steeds.* (Judges 5:22)

After spending the night sleeping on the hay in the barn, Tyler and Danny were up early. Remembering the image of their neighborhood filled with sirens, flashing lights, and police cars, they wanted to put as much distance as possible between them and populated areas where the sickness was most prevalent. Even now, as Tyler looked out the window, they saw someone trying to climb into the pasture near the road.

Tyler shouted and knocked on the door of the little home. Bob came out still dressed in his pajamas. Tyler pointed in the direction of the road. Bob grabbed the shot gun from its wall mount and ran out the door firing the gun into the air. The intruders ran away, but the effort had only bought them a little time. Of this, he was sure.

"Get all the dried food and stuff it in these packs," Bob shouted. "You will need much more than you brought. You can pay the Wilsons back later." After half an hour of going through the cupboards in the house, Danny came out of the house. He was dragging one of the large bags that he had filled. Tyler looked in the bag and saw freeze-dried foods, bars, jerky, and some fresh apples and carrots.

Bob grabbed Little Red's saddle blanket. "I will help you get the horses ready before someone else gets them."

"No, no don't let them get Little Red!" Danny declared.

Tyler had begun to saddle Buck while Bob worked first with Little Red and then with Mr. B.

Danny approached Little Red and stroked her gently as she neighed and nuzzled his pockets. Her velvety soft nose sniffled around for food and tickled Danny. He giggled as he made his way to the little drawer Bob had showed them the previous evening. He took out a couple of sugar cubes. "What about these?" Danny asked. "We have to take these." Danny slipped the entire drawer of treats into a small bag. Then he went looking for something else to carry the oats and the carrots.

After a few unsuccessful tries, Tyler got the blanket and saddle on Buck. When he finished with Buck, Bob had him come over to the huge black. "You need to know how to saddle him before you leave." Tyler stood scratching his head as he looked at the Percheron. The horse looked even larger here in the barn than he had out in the pasture the day before. How would he and Danny manage to put a pack saddle on such a large horse?

Tyler made a couple of throws and managed to get the long leather strap over the back of the horse. Maintaining a distance from the gigantic horse, Danny passed on the other side and grabbed the strap. Tyler came around and gave a sharp pull on it, causing the pack-saddle to land on the horse's back. Mr. B snorted and nodded his head approvingly.

Next Danny had to pass the strap under the horse's belly, which was easy since all he had to do was crouch. "Will he kick me, will he hurt me?" Danny whimpered as he stepped near the giant horse.

"Give him a couple of carrots first," Bob suggested. Danny complied. The horse chomped down the carrots and sniffed Danny expecting more. Meanwhile, Danny quickly reached under the belly of the horse and handed the strap over to Tyler.

To get the pack on Mr. B, the boys hoisted the saddle bag up on the buckskin, then Tyler mounted the buckskin and slid the bags over onto the back of the Percheron. Sitting backward in the saddle, he used the leather thongs on the saddle of the black to secure the bags. Though the bags were heavy, the horse could easily carry them in addition to full-grown man.

Just as Tyler was finishing with Mr. B, Wolf, the wolf-dog, made his appearance and, while wagging his tail, picked up a bag in the corner and brought it over. It was his pack, and he wanted to go with them. If you have a horse-sized dog, then you must have a pack to fit him, Tyler thought.

Now it was time to mount up. Danny was more than eager to get on "his" pony. He went to the left side of Little Red, took hold of the saddle horn in his left hand and the saddle pummel with his right. He put his left foot in the stirrup. Danny pulled and Tyler pushed him up on the horse. Danny beamed. He hadn't looked so happy in weeks. Tyler mounted easily and the little group ventured forth, keeping alert. Danny was talking again, but softly. Little Red snorted, nickered, and tossed her head to the various comments he made. She obviously enjoyed the sound of his voice.

A perfect pair, thought Tyler.

Looking down to the main road, Tyler could see more people trying to get in the gate. At full gallop, Mr. B took off down the entrance road toward the intruders, with his lead rope dragged in the dirt. Once there, he began to snort and rear over the folks while Wolf, growling, went in low. Bob grabbed the gun and fired into the air. Then he handed the gun to Tyler, who secured it on his pack.

The intruders, outnumbered, hurried away while Wolf growled, and Mr. B snorted. After they had returned to the barn, Bob and both boys lavishly praised the animals. Finally, they were underway. Bob locked the gate behind them, unsure how long it would keep intruders out. Everyone was looking for a place to stay away from the city and the threat of the virus.

Bob gave the little group his blessing. Now that his responsibility with the horses was over, he could plan his own trip. He could finish his packing and leave quickly to avoid the quarantine.

After their encounter, Wolf decided to stay with the boys, horses, and most of all with the gun. He trotted along beside the horses. Tyler was eager to get off the main road where they were certain to encounter more bands of marauders looking for supplies. The further they got from the metropolitan areas the better. They took the first side road.

Soon they were on a narrow, winding gravel road that led up the mountain. Patting Little Red, Danny asked, "Do you like being out of your pasture?" As if she understood, she nodded her head up and down, up and down.

While Wolf ran off to chase rabbits, the three horses plodded up the spruce tree-lined road. Circular patches of trees were broken by large fields of grass filled with beautiful white and yellow daisies. The horses enjoyed the change of scenery. They stopped for a mouthful of tempting green grass. When Little Red stopped to graze, Danny slipped off the horse and into the field of flowers.

"I want to give some of these to my mother," he cried as he began picking.

Then he stopped. "I can't hand these to her. Maybe she is in Heaven now." His eyes filled with tears.

He held up the bunch of flowers. "Look, Mom! Do you see these? They are all for you. I love you so much." Danny sobbed.

Little Red seemed to sense Danny's sorrow, and nuzzled his shoulder as he sat on the ground. Desperately, Danny grabbed the little horse's neck and buried his face in her hide. Little Red continued to nicker softly as she attempted to give him comfort. Tyler turned his face away in disgust.

As the horses stood there munching their breakfast, Tyler broke out the breakfast bars. He and Danny had not taken the time to eat. He handed two bars to Danny. "I hope we have left our troubles behind."

Danny smiled as he took breakfast bars from Tyler. "Yesterday I was too tired to walk any farther, then Little Red appeared. Now, look! We have reliable transportation, and it looks like Wolf and Mr. B will protect us. We have some new friends, too," Danny continued to smile. "God and my mom are looking down on us from Heaven, and they are protecting us!"

Tyler scowled at this remark, but he kept silent.

Danny began to tell Little Red all about his school friends and the games they played at school. She enjoyed the sound of his high-pitched voice and nodded her head as if she understood. "Are we going back to school, Tyler?"

"Do you know what 'one day at a time' means?" We have to keep ourselves safe. The world out there has gone to Hell in a hand basket. People are going crazy trying to get what they need to live. We have provisions, water, and transportation. People will want what we have. We will have to be very careful. We have to stay away from people. We do not know who is sick with the virus."

"Do you hear that, Little Red? We have to stay safe." Little Red was quickly filling the empty spot in Danny's heart.

Mr. B let out a snort and nodded his magnificent head. He pawed the air with one of his salad-plate size hooves. Tyler wasn't sure what this horse was, but it was clear that he was much more than a packhorse.

# God vs Nature

May 29th afternoon

*Remember His marvelous works which He has done, His wonders, and the judgments of His mouth.* (Psalm 105:5)

After the challenging start, the day had been uneventful. They had traveled through beautiful green hills, dotted with white and yellow blooms. Here and there, they stopped to let the horses graze for a few minutes. Danny continued to be amazed by the flowers. He picked a blossom and studied it carefully. "Look at this!" Danny exclaimed. "See how God made it so perfect. Each flower has six petals and sticks coming out of the middle. They even smell good."

Tyler snorted. "God didn't do that, nature did."

Danny responded, "Who's nature? I have never heard of her."

Tyler responded with disgust. "Don't you know anything? Nature is all this." He made a sweeping gesture. "It all keeps going year after year. It all evolved from one-celled organisms."

Danny scoffed. "Are you trying to tell me all this beauty happened by itself? Do you think that if we put some dirt on a rock, it would turn into a beautiful flower or a pine tree after a while? Ha! You make me laugh! Take Little Red, for example. (The little mare lifted her head at the mention of her name.) She has wide flat, teeth that are perfect for grinding grass. Wolf has sharp teeth for tearing meat. Do you think they just turned out that way by accident?"

Tyler moaned. "It is no use. You are too young to understand."

Danny seemed to sense that he had the advantage. "Have you ever seen a flower form out of dirt? Have you ever seen it happen? Have you?"

Tyler was angry now. "No one is saying that flowers formed from dirt. First, came the one-celled animals and plants. Then they evolved over millions of years and…"

Danny was ready for that one. "How long do you think it took to make these beautiful petals from one cell."

"Stop talking this nonsense or I'll leave you in this meadow. Don't talk to me anymore. I don't want to listen to your nonsense!'"

Danny climbed up on Little Red and threw his arms around her neck, giving her a big hug. "You understand, don't you, girl?" he whispered to the horse.

Later in the day they entered the security of tall pines. Now the sun had set. Tyler pulled them up into a little grassy area between the trees. He wanted an attractive and secluded area for their first night in the forest. They set up the pop tent quickly and used their foot pump to inflate the air mattress. After a simple supper, they crawled inside.

"I'm scared, Danny whined. I haven't ever slept out here. It is so dark! What are those strange shadows over there? What if a bear or a lion comes? I want my cuddly bear. I want my mommy."

Tyler got up and crawled out of the tent. It wasn't quite dark yet. What could he do to silence Danny? He looked at the horses tied up nearby. He untied Little Red and brought her close to the tent. "Look, I brought you Little Red."

The pony knelt and lay next to the tent, getting as close as she could to Danny. She seemed to sense that he needed her. Danny tried to hug her from inside the tent. With the little horse taking the place of both teddy bear and mommy, Danny was soon fast asleep.

"Wow, smart horse! Problem solved!" exclaimed Tyler. "This may be a long trip. Where does this kid get these ideas about a god making all this stuff?"

Tyler looked out through the canvas opening, at the shadows of the trees and bushes. He heard the cicadas and the occasional hoot of an owl. Off in the distance, he heard a howl. Was it a dog, a coyote, or a wolf? "Where is <u>my</u> teddy bear?" he thought. He got up and retrieved the gun from the saddle. Just then Wolf ran up with a rabbit in his mouth. He sat down near the tent to eat his supper. Tyler grabbed his collar and dragged the dog to the tent entrance. Wolf understood what he had to do. The dog finished his meal and took up his position in front of the tent to protect the boys.

# Learning to Ride



*Harness the horses, mount the steeds!* (Jeremiah 46:4)

The birds began chirping loudly around five o'clock in the morning. Even though the sky was only starting to get light, the birds insisted that morning had arrived.

"Do I have to get up now?" Danny moaned.

"Sleep as long as you can. I'd rather hear snoring than talking nonsense." Tyler slowly pulled himself out of the tent and thought of all the work it would take to re-saddle the three horses. However, the task did not take as long as the previous morning.

Danny got up in time to help with saddling Mr. B. After he finished handing the strap under Mr. B's belly, he offered two sugar cubes to the over-sized horse who munched them happily. All three horses seemed to enjoy the outing, seeing new territory, and getting to know the boys.

They were off to an earlier start than the previous morning. It was almost magical seeing the early morning sunlight filtering through the aspens and pines. All seemed so peaceful and untouched, different from the suburban environment they knew.

They continued on the dirt road for several miles. They felt more confident in their ability as horsemen. It was Danny who nudged Little Red in the side with his heel. The little horse picked up the pace and broke into a very bouncy trot. "Help, how do I make her stop," he called.

"Pull back gently on the reins and say "Whoa," Tyler called back. Danny tried, and it worked. They were back to walking for now, but the door to explore all the mysteries of horsemanship had opened. They had much to learn over the next few days.

# A Chopper!

June 1st

*Though I walk in the midst of trouble, you preserve my life.* (Psalm 138:7)

They made camp by opening their little pop tent in a dry ditch along the road. There had been a powerful breeze, and they wanted as much shelter as possible. Tyler took a rope from his saddle and wound it through a few tumbleweeds. He tied each end to a tree. Then he spread the tumbleweeds along it to provide a wind break and camouflage over their tent.

Both boys were tired and eager to get out of the wind, so they crawled into the tent to munch on their apples, carrots, and dry cereal. Soon they were fast asleep. But the howling wind awakened them. The constant scratching of the tumble weeds on their tent was no help either.

Finally, Tyler got up and untied one end of the rope. By now the wind had risen to gale force. He struggled back into the tent and zipped up the flap. All they could do was wait until the wind died down.

Just before sunrise the wind settled into a brisk breeze. The boys, now exhausted from their nearly sleepless night, fell asleep until well beyond their usual waking time.

It was Little Red who came over and nuzzled the boys. Although they told her to go away, she didn't listen. Soon the other two horses joined in the snorting and blowing around the tent, and Wolf grabbed a flap in his mouth and started to pull.

Danny awoke with a strange notion that something was wrong. He emerged from the tent and began immediately to prepare Little Red for the day's journey. In the process he tried to embrace his favorite horse, but today Little Red would have none of it.

Tyler was giving Danny his boost into the saddle when they heard it: the chop, chop, chop of a helicopter. Even before he could swing his leg over his over, the horses had taken off into the forest where there was no road. They found a dense thicket of bushes and crashed their way into the midst of it. Mr. B folded his legs and lay down in the bushes, breaking several small limbs as he went down. Buck followed suit as did Little Red. Tyler made certain that the broken branches were strewn over them to hide them further.

Tyler and Danny held their breath until they could no longer hear the chopper. Then Tyler started to stand, but Little Red nudged him. Buck pushed him over into the bushes with his muzzle as a second chopper flew over the ridge. This time everyone waited in silence until Little Red finally rose to her feet and made her way out of the bushes to the road.

"Do you think they were looking for us?" Danny asked.

"I think they are looking for everybody who is breaking the quarantine."

"Boy, if they find us, they will take us back to the city, and we won't be able to leave the event center for weeks. Maybe we will be exposed to the sickness, and maybe we will die. What will happen to Little Red, if they take us back?"

"That's why we have to be really careful," Tyler replied.

"I think the animals protected us this time," Danny commented. "No, I think it was God who was protecting us, and He was using the animals."

"That's your theory," Tyler commented. "It is <u>not</u> mine."

# Limping!

June 7th

*Though he may stumble, he will not fall, for the Lord upholds him with his hand.* (Psalm 91:10)

As the horses began to move around in preparation for their saddles, the boys noticed that Little Red had developed a limp. Tyler realized that it would be unfair to make the little horse continue. "Get down, Danny. You can ride behind me. Little Red can stay here. There is lots of grass to eat."

"I will never leave her," Danny cried. I will stay and die with her. I am not coming." He did dismount to protect his pony.

Meanwhile Little Red began to try to scrape her hoof on a rock. Finally, Tyler gently lifted it using her fetlock (a tuft of hair above the hoof) and looked at her horseshoe. A rock was stuck in her frog (the bottom, exposed part of her hoof). Using his knife, Tyler managed to dislodge it.

Once the rock was gone, Little Red began to prance around. She was no longer lame, and she was proud of that fact! After that, Tyler made it a habit to check the hooves of all three horses every day.

As they got on their way, Tyler had a new idea. He had Danny ride Little Red down the road and around the curve. As soon as they were out of sight, he called to Danny to come back and find them. The little sorrel came loping back and took off the main road at the exact place that

Tyler and his mount had left it. Tyler discovered that, when separated, the four animals always found their way back to the others. They would need this trick.

# Dancing and Prancing

June 9th

> *There is a time for everything…a time to weep and a*
> *time to laugh, a time to mourn and a time to dance.*
> (Ecclesiastes 3:1,4)

The horses continued to be full of surprises. Danny had gotten over his saddle sores. The first several days had been a little hard on both boys. But Danny was so enamored with his horse, that he was willing to put up with discomfort to be close to her.

Walking had provided enough excitement for both novice riders on the first few days, but soon they were ready for something more. Danny, remembering his few moments of bouncing on Little Red, urged her into a trot. Tyler clucked to Buck, and the horse also broke into a trot. The Percheron followed suit. "Ow!" Danny cried as he bumped along

"Stand in the stirrups," Tyler called out. Tyler had seen riders "post" during the bouncy trot. The boys practiced that until they had mastered it. The secret they discovered was to have the stirrups at the right length, not too long or too short.

Next, they practiced the gallop, and finally, they dared to allow the horses to run. Little Red, although disadvantaged because of her height, had lots of spirit and tried hard to keep up with the larger horses. Running beside the horses, Wolf barked loudly pretending to be a horse and enjoying the run.

Tyler soon realized with relief that Danny had an inborn knack for horseback riding. He had balance and seemed to anticipate Little Red's moves so that he could stay firmly planted in the saddle. Likewise, Little Red was sensitive to her inexperienced rider, whom she obviously loved and sought to protect. They were an inseparable pair--the bond between animal and child, tight as any Tyler had ever seen. Tyler was pleased that he no longer had to provide entertainment for Danny. Little Red was doing a great job of that. The presence of Little Red reduced his interactions with Danny and that was a welcome change for Tyler.

Meanwhile, Tyler was bonding with the remaining animals. Still annoyed by the constant jabbering of his brother, he admired the quiet strength of Mr. B and the ability of Buck. Wolf was becoming a favorite by proving rabbits for roasting and by protecting the group. The boys were slowly healing from the shock of losing Danny's mother. They both enjoyed riding horseback and exploring the mountain terrain.

One evening they built a small campfire and roasted legs of rabbit in aluminum foil. Wolf had caught the rabbit and was happy to share with the boys. Tyler got out his harmonica and started to play. Mr. B perked up his ears and performed a wonderful gait. His front legs danced while his back legs trotted along. When he finished, Tyler and Danny clapped and pulled out sugar cubes for him. Little Red, not to be outdone, tried to prance around on her back legs, but she fell back to all four legs. Danny gave her some sugar anyway, and then tried his own version of the dance. After a few minutes, he fell in a heap laughing. Next Wolf tried some moves while balancing on his front legs. The boys cheered and clapped.

Now it was Tyler's turn. He pulled out his iPod and risked using some of its precious battery life to provide the music to demonstrate his moves. Obviously, he had been practicing. The horses all snorted approvingly. Only Buck had not shown his talent, but his time would come.

# Uninvited Guests!

June 10th

> *For the Son of Man has come to seek and to save what is lost.* (Luke 19:10)

After that first evening of entertainment, the group had a time of demonstrating their talents every night. Some nights Wolf tried his efforts at singing, or howling. He could go into a high howl, mouth puckered into a circle, head and neck extended like a real wolf. He dropped into a low growl, teeth barred. He didn't seem to have control over the pitch, and he could not reproduce his previous howl/growl combinations.

One evening, after finishing their jam session, they saw the searchlights of an army-green helicopter over a neighboring ridge. Instinctively the boys, horses, and dog backed into the woods. Tyler quickly threw dirt on what remained of the fire. With no light, it would be difficult to see the little group.

The helicopter landed and three men searched with powerful flashlights. Tyler pulled Danny down behind a large rock. He pulled the shotgun from the saddle mount. The men were oblivious to the fact that the animals had snuck up behind them, until they were alerted by a low growl. Turning, they saw a large animal in the darkness. They could just make out the eyes, that seemed to be flaming with anger and horseshoes the size of dinner plates shinning above their head. Then the full weight of the front of the Percheron came down just inches from the first man's head. The second man felt his pants leg in the grip of a mouth of sharp wolf-like teeth. The third man tried to run from a rearing Little Red and turned right into Buck's rear hooves. One of them caught the sleeve of the man's shirt ripping it off.

The men needed no more encouragement. They ran back to the helicopter and took off. "What was that back there?" asked one of the men. "Was it a huge monster with shinning eyes and sharp teeth?"

"We have discovered something that is clearly more frightening than the super virus!" another exclaimed.

Returning to the camp, Tyler used the horses to help him move the gear about one-quarter mile deeper into the forest. After a big round of sugar cubes, dog treats, and carrots for the animals, they all settled down again for a well-deserved night of sleep. That was their last evening of audible entertainment.

# Sickness and Healing

June 11th morning

*He sent forth his Word and healed them; he rescued them from the grave.* (Psalm 107:20)

Danny thought it was the overcast sky that had caused Tyler to sleep in. He had tried to rouse the older boy several times to no avail. Finally, Tyler let out a moan, "Let me alone, I feel sick."

Fear gripped Danny's stomach. Tyler was argumentative and grumpy, but he was all that Danny had now that his mother had passed on. What if he was sick? What would Danny do then? He reached for their canteen. Then with a shudder remembered that they had both drunk from this canteen. If Tyler really was sick, would he be next?

There was no doubt left in Danny's mind when Tyler got up a few moments later and vomited the contents of his stomach. Danny grabbed his knees and closed his eyes tightly. "Jesus, please heal Tyler. I have no one to take care of me. The horses and dog that You gave us are great, but I need a human too. Please heal him!" Danny stayed in this position, rocking back and forth with the intensity of his prayer.

"Whew, I feel better!" Tyler exclaimed. "I guess that when that chopper came last night I grabbed and ate a piece of uncooked rabbit. Yes, I feel a lot better." In a few more minutes Tyler was on his feet and busy packing up their supplies.

Danny breathed a silent "Thank you, God! Thank you, Jesus!" Then joined Tyler with the packing.

# South Park



*I will make all your enemies turn their backs and run.*
(Exodus 23:27)

The group descended Kenosha Pass into the large green bowl known as South Park. Patches of darker green dotted the sides of the bowl. These were stands of aspen trees clumped together by edaphic factors. Above the hills, billows of white clouds were scattered on the blue background of the sky. During the winter this place is the site of blizzards that lift white swirls of snow hundreds of feet into the clear blue sky.

Today the sun warmed the landscape as they made the turn at the bottom of the pass. Several horses from a fenced field nearby greeted the group. They came up to the fence and exchanged snorts with Buck and Little Red. Mr. B joined the group at the fence where he began to sniff the horses. Not liking what he sniffed, he backed up and reared; beating the air with his outsized hooves. The fenced horses snorted in return. A stallion joined the group, his ears laid flat against his head and his teeth barred. He began rearing and bucking.

An old truck, that had managed to find gasoline somewhere, appeared raising a cloud of dust on the unpaved, private road. It screeched to a halt, and a man jumped out, waving his arms and shouting at the group.

"Get away! Take your horses and get out of here! Don't you know that my stallion will jump that fence, and you will have a real fight on your hands?"

Tyler began to pull Buck away while Wolf began barking at the strange horse. Danny managed to get Little Red away. He was obviously in less danger since he was riding a mare. As expected, Mr. B followed the group.

The man got in his truck and started after the group. But, when he saw that Tyler and Danny were kids, his mood changed. He checked out their horses and liked what he saw. He could use these horses now that the virus caused gas to be almost impossible to buy. The delivery trucks and trains were all grounded by the quarantine. He pulled his truck over to the side of the road and walked over to Tyler and Danny and their group. Wolf crouched low and growled.

"Name's Zeke! You boys acted fast. Your big black horse would have drawn my stallion into a real fight. What brings you boys out here today?"

Before Danny could open his mouth, Tyler took up the conversation. "I'm Tyler and this is Danny! We are on a camping trip. My dad and mom should be coming over the pass at any moment. They stopped to pick some raspberries."

The man stared at the boys. He sensed they were lying. "How about you boys come on down to the house and wash up. My wife, Emily, is about to put supper on the table. You look like you could use some good grub. Your folks can catch up with you when they get up this way. Maybe they would like something to eat, too."

There was nothing that the boys could do for the moment, so they followed Zeke to the house. When they reached the corral, at Zeke's insistence, they opened the gate and put their horses inside. They entered the somewhat dilapidated, wood clad, farmhouse. The smell of food cooking on the stove was irresistible.

Emily met them at the door. "We have been lucky here. There have been no cases of the Super Virus. I have heard that there is no way to fight this virus. The antibiotics we all have been taking washed into the rivers and our public water supply. This resistant strain of the virus is immune to our antibiotics. It even appears to grow faster in response to some medications. To stay well we need to avoid contact with everyone. How long has it been since you boys had contact with others?"

The boys assured her that they had been riding alone in the mountains for at least two weeks.

Soon they were sitting at the table enjoying a good meal of fried chicken, mashed potatoes, and gravy. Zeke had an attractive daughter named Liz who about Tyler's age. Neither Tyler nor Danny had talked with anyone for close to a month. They were hungry for food but also for companionship.

After the meal, Tyler helped Liz clear the table. They exchanged their despair with the lack of social media. Danny left the two and went outside to explore the ranch. He went first to the corral to check on Little Red and the other horses then headed out behind the barn. There he overheard Zeke talking to one of the ranch hands.

"We need these horses! It should be simple to get rid of these kids, but how shall we do it?

"I could take the horses while they sleep tonight."

"Nope," Zeke replied. The kid sleeps with his little mare. Besides the horses are inseparable. How about we offer to give them a lift up the pass in the trailer to the last place that they saw their parents. When they get out to look for them, we will drive off with the horses."

"Perfect" the hired hand replied.

Danny crouched behind some bales of hay to make certain that he was not discovered and waited until dark to go back to the farmhouse. He found Tyler and insisted that he come out to the shed where he would spend the night with Little Red.

When Tyler entered the shed, he found Danny curled up next to Little Red. Danny handed him a scribbled note: *They are going to take our horses. They plan to load them up and drive us to the top of the pass, then dump us out to look for our parents while they drive off with our horses. Ask God to keep us safe.*

Tyler took the note and read it fast. Ignoring the prayer, he crumpled it and handed it back to Danny as Zeke entered the shed. Tyler had been tempted to ask to spend the summer with Liz and her family. But, now that Zeke's intentions were clear, he quickly discarded that plan. He would be stuck with Danny for a while longer.

Tyler acted upset that their parents had not caught up with them. Zeke, pretending to be the gracious host, insisted that they stay the night.

Danny curled up with Little Red in the shed while Tyler slept on the sofa in the living room of the farmhouse.

# Saved by Sheep

June 12th

> *For you were like sheep going astray, but now you have returned to the Shepherd and Overseer of your souls.* (I Peter 2:25)

By the time Danny and Tyler finished their breakfast, the men had loaded the horses up in the trailer. When Tyler began to object, Zeke explained.

"Your parents have been spotted on Red Hill Pass. We are taking you and your horses to help you catch up with them. We want to make sure your horses don't get mixed up with our stallion again. Jump in the truck."

Since the horses were already saddled and loaded, what choice did Tyler and Danny have? They jumped in the cab. Danny turned to Tyler and whispered in a low voice, "Wolf is still out there, and he will follow the horses."

Tyler looked intently into the rear-view mirror watching for Wolf. Finally, he saw his grey shape dart across the road about a quarter-mile behind them. He was coming!

The truck pulling the horse trailer started up Red Hill Pass when, suddenly and unexpectedly, the road was blocked by a herd of sheep that entirely filled the road. Zeke got out and, along with his hired man, attempted to drive the sheep off the road, but the sheep merely let the men pass into the middle of the flock, then reformed behind them blocking their way back to the truck. What Zeke did not know was that Wolf had driven the sheep onto the road, and, hidden by bushes near the road, it was he who continued to push the sheep in front of the truck.

Tyler and Danny had been hoping for just such a break. They were out of the cab and around behind the trailer immediately. Tyler boosted Danny up to unhitch the tailgate. Danny darted up between the horses, quickly untied them and coaxed them to back out.

The two men were so involved with the sheep that continued to mill about in front of the truck, that they did not see the boys and horses behind the truck dart into the forest. By the time that they got the sheep off the road, the boys and horses were deep inside the forest. They found a power line that cut through the forest and rode on the cleared area beneath it, making good time and leaving no hoof prints on the grassy slope.

By sunset they had reached the base of Trout Creek Pass. They knew they had escaped this time, but they didn't dare start a campfire that could be spotted by some of Zeke's neighbors in South Park.

# A Truckload of Disease

June 13th

*Now forgive my sin once more and pray to the Lord*
*your God to take this deadly plague away from me.*
(Exodus 10:1)

The next morning brought a change in the weather. The green bowl ended where a gray, cloud-filled sky began. It was raining in the mountains above them.

They were traveling southwest as usual down what seemed to be a deserted road when they came upon a truck that looked to be thirty to forty-years old. The back of the truck was full of people. Some were lying on stretchers and seemed to be quite ill. Some of the people shouted, "Come help us." Others shouted, "Stay away, plague, plague!" "Have you heard of the plague? Some think it is in the water. Others say they caught it from infected folks. There are lots of sick folks in these parts."

"Look," someone cried pointing to the boys and their animals. "They have food!"

Immediately some folks jumped off the truck and started chasing the boys. Now it was time to test their horsemanship. "Go!" shouted Tyler as he dug his heels into Buck's side. "Go," shouted Danny as he did the same to Little Red. Soon they were barreling down the road, leaving the truck and its sickened passengers in a cloud of dust. Mr. B gave a backwards glance occasionally to see if the truck's passengers needed more of a threat to keep them from following. Wolf gave a low-throated growl before he too took off down the road.

Tyler was the first to note that more trouble lay on the road ahead. The bridge had been recently washed out, maybe only an hour or two before they arrived. There had been no warning on the road, probably because there was now no one to post a warning. The river, swollen by recent rains, lay ahead down a steep embankment. They couldn't go back because the truckload of sickened passengers lay behind them. The horses came up to the spot where the bridge had been. There was a drop of about twenty feet down the embankment to the river that was flowing rapidly.

Buck snorted and started down the embankment. A sure-footed horse, he made it to the bottom easily in a series of hops, then without hesitation, plunged into the water. To Tyler's astonishment, they were soon swimming, crossing the swift current. Immediately, Wolf was in the water right beside them. Clearly this was his "cup of tea." In a few minutes, they had safely reached the other side.

Now Mr. B made an entrance into the water. He was not as comfortable with the experience, but his immense size enabled him to walk across with his head above the rushing water, as Wolf barked encouragingly from the bank.

That left Danny and Little Red alone on the bank. Danny had started to cry and Little Red was snorting nervously as she walked back and forth along the riverbank. Without hesitation, Wolf jumped back into the water. He swam back across and, dripping wet, ran up the embankment to Danny and Little Red. He jumped in the air and grabbed Little Red's reins from Danny's hands, then started urging her down the embankment. On the opposite shore, Mr. B neighed encouragement.

With Wolf at her side on the upstream side of the river, Little Red entered the water. She reached her depth and started to go under. But, with Wolf's encouragement, she began to swim, and with difficulty made it to the other side. Danny clutched her mane and the saddle horn tightly and whispered a prayer to Jesus.

It was difficult to tell whether the water on Danny's face was from tears of joy, tears of fright, or river water. They continued down the road at a trot happy in the knowledge that no one in the truck of sickened passengers could follow them. Buck seemed particularly proud of the fact that he had the skills to lead the group through the river.

"Where did all that water come from?" Danny wondered half aloud.

"Must have been a flash flood somewhere upstream. I wish we would get some moisture around here," Tyler complained as Buck's hooves kicked up a cloud of dust.

A cool breeze began to dry their wet clothes, making them feel quite cool for the first time on their adventure. A camping spot with an old pump well was located. Tyler was eager to try it, reasoning that the water from underground would be safer than the water in the many streams they crossed each day.

At first, they pumped the creaky, old well to no avail, but then Tyler remembered to prime it with a bit of their current water supply. They poured just a bit of their precious water in, resumed pumping and were rewarded with an abundant flow of water. Carefully, Tyler used their test kit to test the water for dangerous chemicals and bacteria. Once he knew it was safe, they filled all their canisters and bottles. Last, they pumped water for their animals.

"Wow!" Danny mused, later in the afternoon, "There are a lot of dangers out here. I think Jesus is keeping us safe. He kept us safe from the men in the helicopter, Zeke in South Park, and those sick folks in the truck. He even healed you, Tyler. Thank you, Jesus! Thank you, God."

Tyler tried to ignore the remark, but something or someone was convicting him. He felt troubled in his heart. He wanted to both argue and to acknowledge the truth of these statements. He remained silent.

# Lightning Strike!

June 14th


*He loads the clouds with moisture, he scatters his lightning through them.* (Job 37:11)

The day had begun much as all the others but as the morning progressed the horses appeared unusually nervous. Buck circled several times before Tyler managed to get the saddle on him. A little later Little Red shied at a log, lying at the side of the road almost unseating Danny.

"Hang on!" Tyler cautioned. "They're spooked this morning. Maybe it is something in the air! Thank goodness, they were not spooked the first time we rode them. We would not be riding today."

The horses, in addition to being jumpy, had picked up their pace, and insisted on moving with something that was between a gallop and a trot. No matter how many times the boys slowed them down, they always managed to pick up the pace again.

Danny always enjoyed looking at the sky, and today was no exception. He had been watching a dark area of the sky to the west for more than an hour before he thought to mention it to Tyler. Finally, he noted, "I see lightning over there in the sky." He pointed just as a streak jumped from sky to ground. The rumble of thunder was just barely audible. "Do you think it is coming this way?"

As if in answer to his question, a second flash, much closer than the last, lit the sky. The thunderclap came after just seven seconds, only a mile away! The storm was coming their way, no question about that. In fact, it was upon them. The wind had picked up, and it was difficult to talk over the developing storm. Suddenly a bolt struck a dead tree nearby. Immediately the dried-out tree burst into flame. Another strike hit another tree. Several trees started to burn and drop embers. Little Red pulled on her reins. Tyler saw where she was going and pulled Buck in the same direction. "To the river," he shouted.

The dried forest was starting to burn all around them by the time they reached the river. Other animals were also running from the woods to the river. An elk with a huge rack and a cow elk with calves emerged from the woods and headed for the river.

This time, Little Red did not hesitate to go into the water. In fact, all the horses splashed through the water to the far side of the river. Within minutes the fire came up to the riverbank. They could feel its intense heat. Then an ember landed in Little Red's mane setting her hair on fire. Tyler grabbed the collapsed bucket from where it was tied on the packsaddle and began to throw water on all the animals. Sensing the increased danger, the animals got low in the water as did the elk family and the other wild animals. Tyler pushed Danny totally under dousing his hair and clothes, then followed him to the bottom of the river. Tyler continued to use the bucket to throw water on the group, as the fire jumped the river and began to incinerate the forest on the far side. Now there was a wall of flame on both sides of them.

"Is this like Hell? Danny cried. "Jesus, please help! I don't want to die in Hell," Danny coughed and choked on the smoke.

"Then kick!" Tyler shouted as he helped Danny onto a rock that was covered with water. The water almost covered his body. Danny lay on his back and kicked with his legs that were in a deeper pool of water.

Now the horses began to paw at the water. The result was a mist of water in the air above the river that further protected them from the flying embers. Even the wild animals positioned themselves where they could benefit from the mist.

Tyler seemed to be enraged against this obstacle and determined to defeat it. The hotter the fire got, the faster he threw water with the pail. Finally, after twenty minutes, the fire began to abate on the near side of the stream, and the animals moved back in that direction. In close to forty minutes, it was over. The fire had moved on pushed by the raging wind. The storm had finally begun to produce a little rain which sizzled as it struck the still blazing-hot surfaces.

Tyler and Danny spent the night on the riverbank in the drizzling rain. They were soaked to the skin, but they had survived.

# A Blackened Forest



June 15th

> *I will rescue them from all the places where they were
> scattered on a day of clouds and darkness.* (Ezekiel 34:12)

Morning arrived after very little sleep. They had not even attempted to unsaddle the horses in such horrific conditions. They found the saddles had been damaged and some of their supplies had been ruined by the water. They mounted and started back to the road. The forest was still filled with smoke, and patches of fog dotted a landscape of fallen, blackened trees.

When they reached the road, a new challenge awaited them. The road was littered with blackened fallen trees and was impassable. Tyler looked at the mess, then his resolve seemed to strengthen. He found the harness that belonged to Mr. B and hooked him to the first tree. The horse pulled the tree off the road. They hooked him to the next tree and pulled it off.

Danny scouted ahead to identify the largest trees that had to be moved. It was possible to go around or even over some of the trees.

About half a mile down the road, they came upon the body of a burned-out truck. The truck had the same marking as the one they had encountered before the bridge wash out. Near it appeared to be some bones. As they were passing, a realization came to Tyler: "Here is about where we were when the first bolt of lightning struck. The truck and its passengers must have circled back around to try to intercept us. If the fire had not come…" He didn't finish. He didn't need to. The blackened scene said it all.

Danny was quiet for a few minutes. "Looks like we were protected again." Then he offered: "I feel sorry for these folks. I sure hope that they knew Jesus."

"How could they know Jesus," Tyler responded grumpily. "He lived two thousand years ago."

"No, I mean, I hope that they had prayed and asked Jesus' spirit, the Holy Spirit to come and live in their hearts. Because if they didn't…"

"I've heard that expression, 'ask Jesus into your heart.' What does it mean?" Tyler asked.

Danny was pleased that Tyler seemed interested. "It means that when Jesus comes in, He saves us from our sins and takes us to heaven when we die. If you don't have Jesus, you can't go to heaven."

"Whew!" Tyler breathed. He had questions but was afraid to ask, so he remained silent.

After an hour, they passed through the burned portion of the forest and resumed their normal pace.

# Deluge!



*He made darkness his covering, his canopy around him--the dark rain clouds of the sky.* (2 Samuel 22:12)

They had left South Park for the Collegiate Peaks area near Buena Vista. The sky darkened as it had earlier in the week. More rain was coming.

The boys dismounted and attempted to tie their nearly uncontrollable mounts. The flashes and rumbles of thunder had totally unnerved the horses. Tyler found a little overhang in the cliff just about fifty feet from their path. "Come on! Let's get our stuff and set up camp under this shelf. It will keep us out of the worst of the rain."

Danny yelled back, "You got it! I'm coming with my stuff."

The pop tent was set up and the sleeping bags dragged inside. A couple of wet boys crawled inside the tent and began to pull off their wet clothes. They quickly donned the clothes from their waterproof pack and climbed inside their bags to warm up. The temperature had dropped more than twenty degrees in just a short time.

After an hour, the boys sat up in their bags. The rain continued to pour outside their tent. Fortunately, the rain poured off the raised area on each side of the overhang, protecting the boys and their tent.

"It doesn't show any signs of stopping. Looks like we are stuck here for the night," Tyler commented.

Danny began to whimper. "I don't have my mommy. I'm scared and cold. There is nothing fun to do in here. I'm sad."

Little Red seemed to understand and stopped her grazing in the rain to come over and nuzzle the outside of their tent. Danny rummaged around until he found a carrot, which he reached out of the tent flap for her. "These carrots are starting to dry up," he commented.

"Maybe God will make them plump again in this rain," Tyler offered sarcastically. He looked out gloomily at the continuing storm. "Just my luck, stuck up here on the side of a mountain in Noah's Flood!" He picked up a stone and threw it out of the cave and down the embankment. The storm without had awakened the storm within his own mind. "Where's all that protection you were talking about?" He hurled a stick at Danny and grazed his check, leaving a two-inch-long scratch.

Danny cried louder. It was bad enough to be marooned on the side of a mountain, but he could not even trust his traveling companion. He began to mumble, "Help me, Jesus! Help me, Mom. If you are there, send Jesus to help me." He grabbed the corner of his shirt to stop the bleeding.

For a few moments the rain subsided, the clouds broke apart and a beautiful rainbow appeared. "Wow, look at that!" Danny exclaimed. "God heard my prayer."

But, just as quickly, the clouds closed in over the sun and the rain resumed with even greater intensity.

"Ha," Tyler laughed. "There goes your help from God!"

However, Danny was comforted. He remembered the story of Noah and the rainbow of promise at the end of the story. "This rain will end too," he whispered. "Thank you, God!"

He rummaged around, found some comic books and began to read. Night came quickly to the already-darkened sky. The rain, however, was unrelenting.

# Landslide!

June 17th

*The Lord Almighty will come with thunder and earthquake and a great noise.* (Isaiah 29:6)

Just as it was getting light, a series of rumblings was heard outside their tent. Looking out the open flap they saw a four-foot boulder bouncing down the mountain side. Then a roar came from across the valley. A rockslide was gathering momentum and mass as it made its way to the valley below. The steep hillsides in this area were covered by almost no vegetation, and the talus (broken rock) was loosened by the rain, which acted as a lubricant.

Tyler yelled! "The rain is weakening the loose rock on these steep slopes. Thank goodness our horses are safely tethered away from the base of the slope." Hearing a roar, he glanced around the overhang. A rockslide was headed directly for them!

The slide was upon them in seconds, but the overhang protected them from the falling rock just as it had protected them from the rain. Tyler collected all their valuables and put them under the center of the overhang.

As the morning progressed, the volume of rain began to diminish, and soon the storm was over revealing the sun and a bright, blue sky. Relieved, the boys began to carefully gather their belongings and retrieve their horses. They wanted to get away from these loose talus slopes.

# Mountain Meadow

June 18th

*And we know that in all things, God works for the good of those who love Him, who have been called according to His purpose.* (Romans 8:28)

The boys had headed to lower altitudes to avoid the rock and mud slides. Now they found themselves in a beautiful meadow surrounded by towering snow-covered mountain peaks.

"Wow! Look at all the beautiful wildflowers!" Danny exclaimed as Little Red slowed her pace, and lowered her head to sample a mouthful of mountain grass.

The other horses followed suit and soon all three were happily munching away filling their stomachs.

"This is a good place to camp," Tyler remarked. "It is remote. Not many folks can get up this high, especially with the fuel shortage." He urged Buck forward to a little stream.

"Look!" he called to Danny. "This stream has fish. Now where did I put the fishing rods? Oh, I see one sticking out of the pack on Mr. B."

Within minutes both boys dismounted, removed their saddles, and pulled out their fishing gear. They started sampling the product of this mountain stream. Meanwhile, the horses were only too glad to spend the morning grazing on the tender meadow grass.

By lunchtime the boys had caught several trout and were eager to taste their catch. A small plane flew over the southern part of the valley reminding them that their position could still be seen from the air.

Tyler scanned the hillside closest to their location. It was a north-facing slope. He noticed a dark area partially obscured by a grove of trees. Instructing Danny to stay near the stream, he jumped on Buck and rode about one-quarter of a mile to the hill and started climbing. Within a few minutes, he skirted the grove of trees and had entered the cave. The circular opening in the rock of the hillside was about ten feet in diameter. The remnants of a bonfire were seen on the floor of the cave. A few sticks of wood lay scattered about on the floor.

Tyler pushed the unburned sticks together and threw a few dried leaves on top. Taking out his lighter, he soon had a tiny fire going. The smoke spiraled upward toward the ceiling of the cave. Just then a breeze blew in the cave opening which faced north. The smoke traveled toward the back of the cave and out through another opening.

"Perfect!" Tyler thought. "They won't be able to see our fire." He remounted and rode down to get Danny.

After several trips, they transferred all their equipment and clothing to the cave. Then they sat down to enjoy a nice trout meal, throwing extra pieces to Wolf.

After lunch, they returned to fishing. They skinned the fish and laid the pieces of fish flesh in the sun to dry. They carefully raised the pieces to a branch in a tree to avoid predators during the night hours. The boys enjoyed the peaceful setting so much after the last few hectic weeks that they decided to make camp early and continue fishing. Wolf was also happy about the break, and he went off chasing rabbits and squirrels.

At sunset the sky filled with beautiful orange and pink. Danny sat at the mouth of their cave, whispering "Thank you, God."

"No. God didn't make it. It is caused by diffusion of light through the layers of the atmosphere," Tyler commented dryly. "It is pretty, though." Tyler felt the easing tension in their relationship.

The boys slept well in the partial shelter of their cave and felt so relaxed that they decided to let the horses graze another day. Nowhere in their travels had they found such a beautiful green meadow. After lunch, the boys rolled around in the heavy grass under the trees. They failed to notice a large thunderhead developing behind them. After one lightning strike, the downpour began. Scrambling, they managed to reach the inside of their cave shelter before becoming drenched.

"So that's why the grass is so green here," Danny remarked as the boys sat at the front of their cave shelter. "It gets lots of rain." After about thirty minutes, the rain stopped and the sun came out. When the clouds parted, new snow was visible on the highest peaks.

The boys started a campfire and huddled close to it. They spread their wet clothes on some nearby rocks to dry. As evening came, they were only too glad to enjoy the warmth of their sleeping bags.

The next morning, their clothes were still wet so they laid them in the sun to finish drying. When another thunderstorm came up shortly after lunch, they decided to stay another night.

# Wolf's Friend

June 23rd

*Two are better than one because they have a good return for their labor.* (Ecclesiastes 4:9)

The rain fell intermittently during the night, but most of the next day was dry. Their fourth night in the cave was dry but cool. A morning shower got their fifth day off to a damp start. Having found a good and safe place to camp they were not eager to move on.

As they sat in the cave entrance, Danny remarked, "I haven't seen Wolf around lately, have you?"

"I believe he came up to the cave last night after dark. I will remember to watch for him tonight," Tyler responded.

Another day passed as the boys continued to fish and dry their catch. After dark, both boys were eager to catch a glimpse of Wolf. Had the dog who had been such a faithful companion deserted them?

Around midnight both boys heard howling. "Is that our Wolf or is it a real wolf howling?" Both boys sat up in their beds with their tent flap open. The moon was full so they could see two dog-like shapes coming up the hill toward the cave. Both shapes were nearly at the cave when one of the two animals growled, turned and ran. The other animal came up to the cave and laid down in front of the tent. It was their "Wolf," but what was the other animal that had turned and ran? Neither boy had an explanation.

The mystery of Wolf's companion was the center of their discussion the next morning. Wolf did not seem threatened by the animal, but the animal did not feel comfortable around the boys.

Tyler suggested, "I think Wolf has a lady friend."

Danny was disgusted. "Why does he need any friends. He has us and the horses. He doesn't need any friends."

Tyler smiled, unusual for him. "Remember what you prayed when I was sick, Danny? You said you needed a human." (Tyler had secretly appreciated the remark.)

Danny responded enthusiastically, "Yes, and God answered my prayer! You got better right away!"

Tyler wanted to debate the answer to prayer but was happy to see that Danny was happy. Maybe he did like Danny a bit. He could make a few allowances for Danny's strange beliefs. They made Danny happy.

"Maybe Wolf needs another dog or…" Tyler suggested.

"Or do you think he has teamed up with some dangerous wolf?" Danny asked, his alarm growing.

"We just don't know, but if it had been a dog wouldn't it have come up to our tent? I am going to assume Wolf has a lady friend and I am going to call her Lady. We can watch again for Lady tonight."

Just then the boys saw two animals emerge from the forest. One looked like Wolf. Lady appeared to be smaller than Wolf with slightly longer, darker fur. She tried to stay behind the dog or in the bushes. When she spotted the two boys, she turned and ran into the forest.

When both animals disappeared, Danny asked mournfully, "Will Wolf come with us when we leave, or will he stay with Lady?"

Tyler shrugged. "Wolf has been such a help to us, but we cannot force him to come."

# Boredom!



> *Even youths grow tired and weary, and young men stumble and fall but those who hope in the Lord will renew their strength.* (Isaiah 40:30,31)

The cave shelter that had seemed so welcoming, was becoming boring. First, there were the daily rain showers that forced them into the cave. Danny was tired of reading his comic books. Then there was the constant diet of fish. They were ready for some of Wolf's rabbit. They had grown tired of fishing, flowers, and campfires that produced smoke in their cave.

"Don't you have those memorized yet?" Tyler commented about Danny's comic books. The sense of companionship that Tyler had felt for Danny was gone today. He was irritated and bored by their surroundings.

"They are all I have," Danny moaned. "I never thought I would get so tired of rain."

"Maybe you should ask God to make it stop raining." Tyler suggested sarcastically.

Quietly, Danny did ask Jesus. It seemed that his attention was directed to the horses. They seemed to not mind and even enjoy the rain. Maybe they needed more time to graze on the lush green meadow. Yes, that must be it. They had to stay because the horses needed to graze.

"Well, what did God say?" Tyler mocked.

Danny was silent but he no longer questioned the delay that the rain caused. They were in God's hands, and He was taking good care of them.

As he contemplated the sky, he noticed some clearing near the horizon in the north. Fascinated, he continued to watch. The rain seemed to be letting up. Much to his surprise, the clouds began to part overhead and a shaft of sunlight shone through. Next, a beautiful rainbow spanned the sky.

Danny admired the rainbow. "God's promise!" he whispered.

Within an hour, only a few fluffy cumulus clouds remained overhead. Soon, even Tyler was aware that the storm had departed. He began to get the packs ready for an early departure the following morning.

When morning came, the questions on both their minds was "Where was Wolf? Would he come with them?"

# A Fall!

July 1st morning

> *If one falls down, his friend can help him up. But pity*
> *the man who falls and has no one to help him up!*
> (Ecclesiastes 4:10)

After riding several days, the little group had come to the edge of the Black Canyon of the Gunnison. Danny jumped off Little Red and ran to the edge. "Wow! This canyon looks like it is a mile deep! And it is so black. I'm on the edge! I'm on the edge. Look at me! I'm on the edge!" Danny danced and jumped excitedly.

"Wait!" Tyler shouted. "You are too…"

Danny's foot caught a root that protruded from the soil and, with a scream of terror, he disappeared from view.

Tyler could not believe his eyes! Danny had just disappeared! He ran to the spot where he had last seen Danny and peered over the rim. At first, he saw no sign of the boy. His heart beat rapidly. He couldn't lose Danny. Not after all they had been through. Sure, Danny had some weird ideas, but he was also quick to help Tyler if he could. Upon closer examination, he saw a fresh track in the dirt extending downward from the canyon rim. The track disappeared behind a protruding rock. Then he heard it! Sobbing.

"Danny, are you all right?" Tyler called anxiously. All animosity that he had for his stepbrother had disappeared. There was no answer, but the sobbing continued. Tyler ran along the rim trying to get a view of the boy. Obviously, he had not fallen all the way down.

Rounding a little bend in the steep canyon wall, Tyler saw him huddled on a little ledge beneath the protruding rock about ten feet below the canyon rim. He shouted to get Danny's attention, but Danny was holding his ankle and continued to sob. Tyler ran back to the spot where he had last seen Danny. What could he do to save his brother? The canyon wall was too steep for him to crawl down to Danny.

Tyler did what he had never done before: he prayed. "God, if you are there, help me save Danny!"

Tyler waited in silence. After a few moments, the sobbing stopped. "Tyler?" The second time his name was louder, then he heard it loud and clear.

"Yes, yes, I am here!"

"Tyler, I can't move."

"Don't you dare move."

Tyler jumped up and got his horse. Buck had once been used for cattle roping in rodeos across the state. Maybe he could use that skill now. He located their rope tied to the horse's pack.

Bringing the horse and the rope closer to the canyon edge, he made a large loop in the rope and tied it with a slip knot. "I am going to throw a rope to you. Put it around your waist."

Tyler tied the other end of the rope to his saddle horn. He then wound several loops and tied them to shorten the rope. Bringing Buck about five feet from the canyon rim, he threw the free end over the rim in Danny's direction. "Too far to the right" came the words from the canyon.

Tyler pulled the rope up and threw it again. "Stuck on the rock."

Tyler prayed, "Help, Lord." Then he threw the rope again.

"I got it!"

"Put it around your waist and pull the knot tight. Now grab it with both hands."

Tyler looked at Buck who was snorting and pawing the earth. He seemed ready to go. "Pull, Buck," Tyler yelled, "Pull!"

Buck began to back up to pull the slack out of the rope. Once he felt the resistance on the rope, he began to pull in earnest.

Tyler was letting the rope pass through his hands. He would hold it, if it started to slip. Peeking over the rim, he saw Danny's body emerge from behind the rock and start to slide up the canyon wall. Whenever Danny's right foot struck a rock, he tried to push to help himself in his journey. At last, Tyler was able to reach Danny's hand and pull him over the edge.

Buck continued to pull until he had pulled Danny about five feet from the rim. Then he walked forward to where Tyler was helping Danny out of the rope. "Ow! That hurts." Danny pointed to a big scrape on the inside of left leg. It was bleeding.

Danny tried to stand. "Ow!" "My ankle hurts."

Danny was hurt but he was safe! "Answered prayer?" Tyler wondered.

# A Sprain!



*For he will command his angels concerning you…they will lift you up in their hands so that you will not strike your foot against a stone.* (Psalm 91:11,12)

Danny collapsed back on the loose dirt near the canyon rim. "Ow!" he cried. "My leg hurts." His eyes filled with tears.

The scrape on the inside of his leg would prevent Danny from riding Little Red until it healed. Tyler examined Danny's ankle. It was not broken but was certainly badly sprained. Danny could put no weight on it.

Tyler was perplexed. They were not close to any medical facility, and they could not travel in Danny's condition. What would they do? Wow! He thought. I better pray. We got him out of the canyon but now what do we do? As he began to pray, he got the impression that the tent could be set up right where they were.

He got up and looked around and discovered a clump of pinyon pine nearby. He pulled the camping supplies out of the packs still on Mr. B and set up the tent. Next he went to where Danny was still lying on the ground. Standing behind Danny he managed to get him in a standing position. Then, with one arm around Danny and Danny's arm over his shoulder, they managed to walk three-legged style to the tent where Danny dropped to his knees and crawled inside. Tyler cleaned and dressed his abrasion and wrapped his sprained ankle. As soon as he was able, Danny plopped down on his sleeping bag and air mattress. He whimpered a bit, then fell asleep.

Tyler scurried around unloading the horses and letting them graze on the meager grass and weeds in the area.

"Whew!" Tyler thought. "Good thing the horses have had plenty to eat in the last few weeks. Food is going to be harder to come by here." It crossed his mind that it was good that they had been detained by the rain in the mountain meadow so that the horses could store up belly fat and the boys had a good supply of dried fish.

He pulled several granola bars from the pack. Then he crawled into the tent to join Danny. It was still light outside, but it had been a rough day.

Here in this canyon country, the temperatures reached ninety degrees most days in July. The boys would be sleeping on top of their bags and hoping for a cool breeze. Tyler listened intently to the myriad of sounds in this new and different location. There were the familiar cicadas and crickets, but the sound of the rushing water more than 2,000 feet below them was new. The summer breezes whined and whistled as they made their way through the twists and turns of the canyon.

Tyler shivered. The memory of Danny's fall was still fresh in his mind. Were they safe here? Did they need to get up and move their tent farther from the canyon rim? He got up once to reassure himself that they were a safe distance from what could be a fatal fall into the canyon depths. Tyler was now convinced beyond all doubt of the importance of Danny's companionship.

Danny had searing pain to endure. At times, he merely whimpered. Changing position caused him to let out a scream of pain that fully awakened Tyler who was just starting to doze off. It was hours before the boys were able to sleep.

Danny woke up with a start. He rolled over and pain had shot up his leg. He could move his toes and put a little weight on his foot, but there was so much pain. Had he broken something? Exhaustion helped him fall back to sleep.

# Throwing Rocks!

July 3rd

*There is a time for everything... a time to scatter stones and a time to gather them.* (Ecclesiastes 3:5)

When the light of morning awakened the boys, Tyler could not wait to approach the canyon rim and look into its depths while the first rays of the sun illuminated it. At first the canyon seemed to be filled with a churning mist--moisture that had accumulated over-night. Then as the sun sent its rays to dispel the mist, a rainbow appeared. Tyler grabbed his phone and captured a couple of photos. The phone had not been charged since the night in South Park.

By the time Tyler returned to the tent hidden in the grove of pinyon pines, Danny was calling for help. He was unable to stand without help. Once on his feet he hopped to a rock where he sat and planted his one good leg firmly in front. "What am I going to do," Danny cried. I can't ride Little Red, and I can't even walk." Tears began to flow.

"Get better," Tyler remarked. It wasn't that he had no sympathy for Danny's condition. He just did not know what else to say.

Danny crawled back in the tent and fell asleep. Tyler soon joined him. It had been a rough night for both boys.

It was Wolf that awakened them making his first appearance in several days. He brought a half-eaten rabbit and dropped it at their feet. Wolf appeared to be exhausted. He lay down and was soon asleep. Tyler dug a little hole and dropped the rabbit in. Neither he nor Danny were going to eat any part of that rabbit, but Wolf would need it later. Never before had Wolf appeared to have such meager results from his hunt. Was he sharing his food with Lady? The boys had seen no sign of her.

The boys' food supply was limited. Fortunately, they had a sack full of dried fish. They still had some cold cereal, granola bars and beef jerky. It would have to be enough for now.

On the second day Danny managed a few steps after Tyler helped him to his feet. He looked around wondering how to amuse himself.

"I am going to pray," Danny cried as he cradled his face in his hands.

Finishing his prayer, Danny picked up a small rock and tossed it toward the canyon. Then he picked up another rock and propelled it toward the same target. "Wow!" he exclaimed! "I am getting better!"

Tyler took up the contest throwing his rock farther than Danny's, but it went off to the side. "We need a target," he exclaimed.

He dragged over a log. "Let's aim for the middle," he suggested. Soon he and Danny were throwing rocks everywhere trying to hit the target. They picked up skill with each throw.

Then, they tried bigger rocks, flatter rocks, sticks, and pinecones. They tried with their left hands as well as their right hands. They were competing with each other and with their own best efforts. As the sun prepared to disappear behind the horizon, Danny suggested, "Let's mark the locations of our best throws and try again tomorrow."

They crawled into their tent and, as they had done the previous night, enjoyed a supper of dried fish. Danny awoke several times crying in pain, but he got more sleep than the night before.

After a couple of nights in the tent, the boys decided to allow the soft desert breeze to blow on their faces. They pulled the sleeping bags out and packed the tent. When darkness finally came, bringing with it the short summer night, the boys were treated to a spectacle they had never seen before: Thousands of stars were visible in the dark night sky. With no city lights to dim them, the stars shone brightly.

Danny tried to see outlines of figures in the star patterns. "Didn't God do a good job of making all these stars"

"Ha!" Tyler laughed. "These all came from the Big Bang."

Danny was persistent: "And God caused the Big Bang. He did a beautiful job. There must be thousands."

"More like billions," Tyler muttered. "But they are beautiful."

Fatigue took its toll and the boys were soon asleep, lulled by the gentle breezes.

The next morning, Danny grabbed his saddle. He was ready for more adventure. "Let's try throwing from horseback." Danny suggested

"Are you sure you can ride?" Tyler asked.

Danny's ankle was better, but he still had a limp. He mounted Little Red cautiously from the right side. He put his right foot carefully in the stirrup, then swung his left leg over the back of the horse. This was opposite the way he usually mounted Little Red. She pretended to nip him in the leg to show her disapproval. He held his left leg at an angle so that the saddle did not rub the scrape on his leg. Tyler handed him a stone. Danny nudged Little Red ahead, and as she was passing near the target, Danny threw his stone. He circled around to get another stone from Tyler. This time Little Red was at a full gallop by the time Danny tossed the stone at the target.

Now it was time for Tyler to show off his skills. He loaded a sack of stones onto Buck's back then mounted and circled past the target throwing his first stone at his closest approach. Danny approved Tyler's efforts and the boy made another round. By sundown both boys had sore arms, but the log target was nearly destroyed by the many stones that hit it.

"That's enough for today," Tyler declared as he carefully helped Danny dismount. We can have another go at it tomorrow, then we should be on our way since you are comfortable in the saddle again. Tonight, it is clear so we will have another opportunity to view the stars.

However, the next morning both boys had sore arms and suspended the stone throwing for the day.

The following day the competition began again with a new stone target. Both boys were becoming accurate, a skill they would use in the future.

At last it was time to leave the canyon rim. The boys left with regret. They had grown accustomed to enjoying views into the canyon at various times of the day. They loved viewing the stars from this remote place. They circled by the rim one final time then gave their mounts a nudge in the ribs, and the group was on the road again. Wolf was quick to join them although he had been off doing his own thing for much of the summer. There was no sign of Lady.

# Attack!

September 13th

*Your servant has killed both the lion and the bear...*
(I Samuel 17:36)

The group had crossed the mountains of Colorado and were in the Delta area. The mountains had changed to low, rolling hills. The scrub oak and pinon pine were limited to the northern slopes. The south slopes were covered with grass and a few prickly pear cactus plants. As they entered the western part of the state, they dropped in altitude. Even so as night fell, a cold wind started to blow.

Tyler was eager to find a place out of the wind for the night's camp. An over-hanging ledge under a sandstone arch seemed to offer the perfect spot.

They freed the horses from their loads, and set up the tent. Danny was able to help some with the camp setup in spite of his injuries. They decided not to start a campfire because of the danger of drawing attention to themselves. The tent was under the rock. Their food and supplies were pulled up in a tree as usual. Danny fell asleep with a piece of beef jerky in his hand.

Once they had settled in for the night, they were awakened by a thud that seemed to come down right on top of them. A screech and a snarl from Wolf awakened all of them. The horses snorted in fear. Mr. B was rearing. His huge hooves were flailing in the air and reflecting the moonlight.

Tyler quickly found his flashlight. What he saw amazed him. A large cat, maybe a cougar or a mountain lion had attacked them. Wolf had him engaged but the cat was a good match for him. They were going around and around in a ball of fury on the ground. Another dog-like figure stood growling a few yards away. Meanwhile, Mr. B was trying his best to land his now-famous deadly blow. Before he could land the knock-out blow, the cat managed to inflict a deep scratch on Mr. B's leg.

Immediately, Danny and Tyler picked up stones from their assortment near their beds and began heaving them at the big cat. Several stones hit their mark. The cat disappeared into the night.

It was over as quickly as it had started. The boys, Little Red, and Buck were unhurt, but the wolf dog and the Percheron had each suffered a serious wound. Shinning the light on Mr. B's leg, Tyler was astonished to see blood squirting from the gash. Calling to Danny, he pulled off his shirt and tied it tightly around the leg covering the wound. "Hold this on the cut and push down hard." When Danny hesitated, Tyler yelled, "Now!" Next, he took off his belt and wrapped it tightly around the leg above the wound.

Danny, impressed with the urgency of the situation, grabbed Mr. B's leg and squeezed it with all his strength. He could see that the big horse's flesh was quivering. In the light of the flashlight Mr. B's eyes were wide in terror. This only made Danny squeeze more tightly.

"Is Mr. B going to die?" Danny cried.

"Count to 100 and keeping pushing hard on the wound. Don't you dare let any blood out!" Tyler commanded. Danny knelt down near the horse's huge leg, pushed hard on the wound and started to count. After a few dozen numbers, he stopped. "What if…"

"Count and push!" Tyler shouted again.

"But…"

"Push and Count!" Tyler was now frantically fishing around in the saddle bags. At last he had found the first-aid supplies.

"Ninety-nine, 100".

"Count again. Start at one!"

"Do it again. Now!"

Danny finished the third count. Tyler removed his shirt from the wound. He noted with satisfaction that the flow of blood had stopped at least temporarily. He sprayed the disinfectant, and pain killer on the leg. Immediately the horse's flesh stopped quivering, and he gave out a low nicker as a "thank you!" Tyler wrapped the leg firmly in gauze and taped it as tightly as he could. He knew that he should probably ice the wound, but there was no opportunity to do that here.

Next he turned his attention to Wolf, who stood whimpering with the top of his ear nearly severed and hanging at a crazy angle.

"I need you to help me with Wolf," Tyler called. Danny came immediately although he was limping and gagging mildly from the sight of so much blood. Tyler sprayed the wound while Danny cut off strips of the tape that Tyler applied to the ear, repairing it as well as he could.

The sky was getting light when they finally fell back asleep.

# Yellow Leaves!

September 15th

> *Pray that your flight will not take place in winter...*
> (Matthew 24:20)

It was hours before they got underway again. They had shifted much of Mr. B's load to Buck. Even Wolf was required to carry supplies. As they rode along something was stirring in Tyler. Voicing his concern to Danny, he lamented, "We can't go on forever on our own out here in the wild. The animals have been protecting us, and we have helped them, but..."

Danny was quiet for a few minutes, unusual for him, then he ventured, "Do you believe in God now? Don't you think God is using the animals to protect us?"

Now it was Tyler's turn to be quiet. "I don't know. It seemed like God helped me rescue you from the canyon. But there are so many bad people. If there was a God, there wouldn't be bad people."

"But what if bad people make God sad? What if God gave everyone a choice to be good or bad because He wants them to choose Him, not be a slave to Him. Mom believes in God!" Danny turned in the saddle to look at Tyler, who rode behind him.

"You mean your mom believed in God. She's your mom, not mine. She believed, but now she's gone! So much for belief!"

"But what if she is with Jesus, and she is helping Him watch out for us and keep us safe?"

"How could God let this happen? A bunch of people get sick all over the country. Then because there is no transportation, there is nothing for the rest of us to eat, drink, or use for our lives. What's next? Does God hate everyone?"

"But we are not sick or starving. Even some of our electronic stuff still works. Maybe God is showing us that He loves us."

Tyler had no answer. Part of him wanted to accept Danny's simple faith, but his mind kept coming up with objections.

September had been unseasonably warm and much dryer than usual. Tyler was glad for the unusual weather, but he was about to find out that there was a cost to pay. Standing on a hillside above a narrow valley, they were allowing the horses to graze. A stiff breeze was blowing: another common weather component. As usual, Wolf was off somewhere killing rabbits or other rodents, or visiting his lady. They both had seen her during the attack.

They had been riding for about four months now. When his ankle was not hurting, Danny could now scramble up on Little Red with the greatest ease. They both had opportunities to ride bareback (without a saddle) and knew and understood their horses' temperaments and moods.

Danny had been noticing the progression of the fall color. First, back in early September, it had been just an orange leaf here or there. Then it had been the tops of the trees. Finally, the whole forest was engulfed in beautiful glowing reds, oranges, and yellows. Then the leaves began to fall. What fun that provided! Tyler could not count the number or times they stopped to jump in the leaves or the number of times they had pitched their little tent on top of a pile of leaves. "Crunchy!" Danny had noted.

"Look at the beautiful yellow and orange leaves! Don't you think that God made them?"

"I learned that in the fall the green chlorophyll goes out of the leaves and so their yellow color shows up."

"But that doesn't mean that God doesn't make it happen. If God doesn't do it, who does?"

Danny continued, "I just want to say thank you, God for making all the pretty leaves, and for keeping us safe, and giving me Little Red, (the horse was nodding her head) Mr. B, Buck, and Wolf. And especially for giving me my brother, Tyler, who knows so much about the colored leaves, the clouds and the sky!"

Tyler was about to respond with his usual denial of being Danny's brother, but Danny's remark about Tyler's knowledge stopped him. "Why thank you, Danny," he said with unusual warmth. Tyler had a developing interest in science sharpened by this outdoor adventure.

Tyler's attention returned to the leaves. "Those yellow leaves mean cold weather is coming. If it snows out here, we may freeze."

"Or God may protect us just like He has so far."

Tyler signed. He had a growing concern about the coming winter knowing they would never be able to survive without shelter. His plan had been to head south, so that is what they had done. Watching for the shadowless side of the trees, they had headed in that direction whenever the back roads had permitted it. Now, it was getting colder, and they were still in Colorado. There was no one to ask which way to go. Had they finally run to the end of their luck? The next day might prove that one way or the other.

Tyler thought again about Danny's assertion that God was helping them. Certainly, like even the previous evening, many things had worked in their favor. Still, would they even be in this unthinkable situation with no parents and no adults to guide them if there was a God. Why had all this happened? Why had an enemy been allowed to do this--to destroy their country? Immediately, almost as if in answer to his question, scenes from a TV show he had recently watched flashed across his mind. He knew that what he had seen was wrong, yet he had come to accept it and had thought little about the scene at the time. Had his country strayed away from God? An extra loud gust of wind howled through the pines, and Tyler shivered.

# Snow!

September 16th morning

*He says to the snow, "Fall on the earth," (Job 37:6)*

Buck and Mr. B had been snorting and pawing the ground for about ten minutes, when Tyler finally dragged himself out of the tent where they had spent a cool night. Little Red trotted up and began to pace with the others.

Tyler dragged the saddles out of their hiding place and began their morning routine. Danny had learned which parts of the routine he could safely do by himself and started right in to help. Within a half an hour, the horses were saddled, the tent and other belongings were packed, and they were ready to depart.

When Danny tried to mount Little Red, he found her so eager to get started that she would not stand still. Finally, with difficulty he brought her around to a log that he could stand on and climb up. Tyler was having the same problem with Buck while Mr. B, once he had his pack, took off down the road at a gallop ahead of the others.

First light was just appearing in the eastern sky when the two saddle horses caught up with the Percheron. The wind had eased a bit, and the forest seemed hushed with the onset of dawn.

A couple of hours later as they made their way up the slopes of the Uncompahgre Plateau, they could not help but notice that their day was not warming as usual. In fact, the wind was definitely picking up and getting colder. Tyler pulled the heavy winter coats out of their pack. They were only too happy to put them on.

"Why do you think there are so many shapes of mountains," Danny asked. "These are flat like tables, but some look like slides from a playground, and some are pointed like the roof of our house. Don't you think God had fun making all the different shapes?"

"No," Tyler countered. "They were eroded by the wind and water."

"But," Danny questioned. "Why did the wind and water make so many different shapes?"

"Well," Tyler continued. "There were different conditions. Sometimes the rocks were formed on a flat lake or ocean bed. Then they were uplifted and tilted…"

Danny interrupted, "So God tilted the rocks, or made them lie flat, or…"

"No, it was internal forces in the earth that caused it."

"And God made the internal forces in the earth."

Tyler shook his head in dismay but said nothing.

"Look at those clouds," Danny exclaimed changing the subject. "They look like a lot of sheep. There are a lot of white sheep, and some of the sheep are sort of a gray-purple color. What causes that?"

"The dark clouds have more water in them. That is all. The light can't get through."

About an hour later, Danny had another comment. "Now look at the clouds. There are more dark clouds than white clouds, and all the dark clouds have huddled together into one huge pile of darkness. What does that mean?"

"It means that we need to get out our slickers, our raincoats, and get them on pronto." Tyler began to rummage among the packs that were not in their usual places because Mr. B was not carrying his full load. Finally, he located the raincoats.

As they were putting on the slickers, a gust of wind came up. It was a tail wind for them since it was a wind out of the north while they were still headed south. It was difficult to get the yellow coats on and pull them down against the saddles. The coats flapped in front of their faces at times blocking their views.

Just before noon, the rain began. First, there were only a few drops of rain, then more, and finally the rain was pounding them. Not a gentle drizzle but a driving rain: flying water born by the wind. They had never experienced a rain like this. When they turned toward the wind, it threatened to drown them. Both boys had learned to swim. Tyler was on the swim team, but that was no preparation for this. Danny had a zippered hoodie under his winter coat. He zipped it up completely covering his face. The hood of his coat offered additional protection. To make matters worse, the temperature began to fall.

Off to the right, a small lake with wind-whipped waves was providing a landing place for a flock of geese. Through the mesh on his hoodie, Danny watched the big birds land gracefully, then flap their wings before folding them neatly and beginning to swim.

The horses seemed less bothered by the rain, and more energized by the arrival of the storm. They were unstoppable, refusing to respond to the bit. Once when Tyler had reigned Buck up and refused to give him slack in the reins, Buck had turned his head and nipped Tyler's leg. Surprised, Tyler dropped his hold on the reins, and they were off once more.

They could barely see where they were going, but Little Red seemed to know and turned off on a side road. It led past several cabins, all of which seemed vacant and forbidding. Tyler pulled out a shirt and used it as a towel, then caught up with Danny and Little Red. He offered the shirt just as the horse bolted forward nearly knocking Danny to the ground. Little Red had changed from a bouncy trot to a dead out run. Still her shorter legs made it possible for the larger horses to catch up with her.

They crouched low in the saddles, giving their horses free rein as they struggled against the wind-driven rain. At times, the road took them straight into the rain. At other times, the rain was at their back giving them a brief respite.

"My pants are getting wet," Danny whined. "My shoes and socks are wet, and my feet are getting cold."

Tyler looked at the boy's slicker. It did not quite cover his legs and feet when it was stretched over the horse. His own slicker was too short as well. "Mine, too!" Tyler replied.

"When are we going to find a house?" Danny cried, his salty tears beginning to mix with the rain drops making little streams that flowed down his cheeks. "My shirt is getting wet, too."

"Mine too," Tyler responded ignoring his question about shelter. It wasn't that he was ignorant of their situation. He just had no answer.

"I'm going to pray," Danny cried in a pitiful, quivering voice. The increased force of the wind and the storm absorbed his cries as it engulfed the boys, and their animals.

While Tyler could not hear his brother's prayer, God did!

As suddenly as it had come, the rain changed to snow. At first it was a relief not to have the pounding rain. That offered them some respite, but their visibility was still very limited. Little Red, however, forged ahead. She seemed to recognize the area, and to be familiar with the terrain. The other animals struggled to keep up. The horses continued to plod along, heads lowered to protect their eyes, and not stopping to graze as was their custom. Suddenly Little Red began to pick up the pace. Her head came up, her ears tilted forward, and she gave a soft nicker and began to stretch her short legs into a canter and then into a full gallop. The road before them was rapidly disappearing as every feature of the countryside was covered in a blanket of white. One could not even determine where the road was between the trees, but Little Red clearly knew where she was going.

The driving snow was beginning to plaster every object with white. Even the figures of the boys and the horses were difficult to discern from the trees and bushes all plastered with snow.

Tyler was getting concerned. Buck had slid a couple of times on the snow that was changing to ice on the gravel road. He was separated from Danny. This he knew. He was unable to tell if he and Little Red were just ahead or if they were even on the same road. To make matters worse it was getting dark. Tyler looked up. "I need help, now!" he said to the only One who could possibly hear him.

# Shelter in a Storm



*When it snows, she has no fear for her household for all
of them are clothed…* (Proverbs 31:21)

About a half mile down the road, Little Red slowed her pace and turned into a narrow lane that wound up the hill for about a quarter mile. Suddenly, out of the white, swirling mass the shape of a small, brown, log cabin emerged. Little Red trotted confidently up the drive. The small cabin tucked in among the trees meant only one thing to the storm-ravaged horse. Shelter!

In a momentary lull in the wind, the snow settled and Tyler could see. There ahead of him was Danny. The other horses seemed to gain confidence from being rejoined to Little Red and picked up their pace. Danny had dismounted, and Little Red was standing trying to shake off the extra snow. Danny was using his flashlight and punching random numbers on the keypad controlling the garage door. "I know how this works!" he exclaimed.

"Wait," Tyler yelled. "You don't know the combination!"

"My dad showed me how to do this," Danny announced proudly as he continued to punch random numbers. When there was no response, Danny prayed, "Help, Jesus! I guess I don't know how to do it." Suddenly, as if by magic, the garage door came to life with a groan and rolled open. The horses and riders needed no formal invitation to rush inside. For the first time in hours, they were out of the wet and wind. Only Wolf seemed to be content to remain outside. He bounded up the hill tracking a rabbit or looking for his lady. Now that they had found shelter, dinner and companionship were on his mind.

Once inside, Tyler began pulling off the saddles and stacking them on an exposed railing. He asked for Danny's help, but the boy sat huddled in a corner grabbing his freezing feet.

"Danny, Come on! I need your help!"

"I'm too tired…just want to sleep…"

"No! You must not, not now!" Tyler pulled at the door leading to the inside of the cabin. It came open easily. He dragged Danny inside.

"It's still cold in here. My feet and legs hurt."

Tyler began undressing the boy, pulling his shirt over his head, and his pants off. Much of his skin was bluish-white. Tyler tried to focus. He was feeling very sleepy. Maybe a few winks wouldn't hurt. But a voice seemed to come from inside, "No, No, No! Keep moving, keep moving!"

Tyler knew the dangers of hypothermia. They were close to being safe, but not close enough. In the fading light that filtered into the cabin from between the shutters locked over the windows, he could make out a fireplace. The fire had been laid with logs on the bottom, kindling wood, and newspaper on the top.

He returned to the garage and managed to retrieve their matches that were still safe and dry in the little, metal cylinder. Next his hands located their flashlight in one of the saddle bags. Using these two things, he was able to get a good fire going in the cabin. It provided light but at first seemed to do little to overcome the chill that had permeated the place.

Tyler focused the flashlight on the walls revealing Indian blankets, tapestries, and fancy saddle blankets. He was about to take some of those, but his eyes then lit on a narrow ladder with a rope hanging down. A pull on the rope caused the ladder to descend with a creaking sound. Tyler stuffed his flashlight in a pocket and slowly pulled himself up the ladder. In the balcony, he found two beds complete with pillows and warm, fluffy blankets which he quickly threw over the balcony. They landed near Danny.

The sleepy child grabbed a pillow, stuffed it under his head, and fell fast asleep. Tyler descended the ladder carefully. He scooted Danny nearer to the fire and wrapped him in a blanket.

Then and only then did he remove his wet clothes and wrap himself in blankets. He crept over to make a final check on the sleeping child. Danny was resting peacefully. Tyler pulled the blankets off his legs and feet. They still looked white. He carefully touched the skin on Danny's lower leg. "Still feels cold."

Danny stirred and called out the name of his horse, "Little Red, Little Red."

Tyler went to the door that led to the garage and opened it softly as Danny continued calling for his horse, "Little Red, Little Red."

The pony approached the door, hesitated, then stepped up into the house. There was no way to hush the clatter that her small hooves made on the wood floor. She walked slowly as Tyler shown the flashlight on the still-sleeping form of his brother. Then, as she had done so many times before, she knelt, front legs first and back legs following beside his small form. He reached out one arm and hooked it over her neck, snuggled closer, and fell back asleep.

Of course! Little Red's body heat! Tyler grabbed a blanket and snuggled with Little Red on the opposite side.

About an hour later he was awakened by a sharp bark and scratching on the door. When he went to investigate, he found Wolf standing outside with two freshly killed rabbits dangling from his mouth. Tyler took the two rabbits, and the dog was off again with a bound. Another dark dog-like shape was just barely visible between the trees. Lady? Tyler could not help noticing the three inches of fresh snow and the near-blizzard conditions outside.

Tyler felt a little better after the nap and focused on starting a fire in the kitchen stove. Like the fireplace, the fire had already been laid. Sticks of wood rested on lumps of coal. Newspaper had been stuffed around the wood in the firebox. Tyler retrieved a single match from the canister in the cupboard. He struck the match quickly on the iron surface of the stove and dropped it into the firebox. The newspapers burst into flame and soon even the coal was producing warmth for the chilled room.

Next, Tyler found a large pot. There was no running water in the cabin, but he took the pot outside and scooped snow from a six-inch drift that had formed near the garage door. He placed the snow-filled pot on the stove and began skinning the rabbit legs. They were added to the boiling water on the stove.

# Rest and Relaxation

September 18th

*He who dwells in the shelter of the Most High, will rest in the shadow of the Almighty.* (Psalm 91:1)

It was nearly noon of their second day in the cabin. Light filtered in through two windows on the leeward side of the cabin. They had left the other windows covered with shutters to protect against the biting wind that was still blowing and the blizzard-like conditions that still prevailed outside. The two boys lay on the oval rag rug near the fireplace playing an old Monopoly game they had found near the wood box. The fire in the fireplace provided both warmth and light and gave a cozy feel to the room. Behind them, in the kitchen, the cook stove was also providing warmth and the delicious odor of cooking rabbit stew. Wolf had provided his usual contribution of rabbit legs, while Little Red had nosed around in the garage and uncovered two barrels filled with dirt-covered potatoes, onions, and carrots. Little Red and the other horses had each accepted the offer of an unwashed carrot, but the other vegetables did not interest them. Instead they munched happily on the bales of hay that had been placed around the garage for insulation. Tyler had added some of the potatoes, onions, and carrots to his stew. He had made enough to last for several days. In addition, the kitchen cupboards had some dry cereals, crackers and cookies they could munch on.

Danny rose and stretched his legs. He had obviously recovered fully from his ordeal with hypothermia of the day before. His ankle had also nearly fully recovered. A few days of rest was all that it needed. He walked around examining the room's contents. The exposed logs of the walls were partially covered with Navajo blankets, a colorful saddle blanket, and a small rag rug lay on the floor. He asked about the rag rug.

"It is made of pieces of cloth from worn out shirts and pants. Someone has woven all the pieces together to make the rug." Tyler explained. "Look at these quilts," he continued. "See the pieces of cloth in them? They were probably made from pieces of new cloth. I remember seeing one on the bed at my grandma's house." Tyler had neatly stacked the folded quilts on top of their sleeping bags and pillows in the old rocker. They would use them again this evening.

Tyler looked intently at the relief map hanging near the kitchen window. Someone had placed a small push pin in the map to show the location of the cabin on the map. As he had expected, they were in the higher terrain, southwest of Delta. They were going to have to lose altitude and travel farther south to get relief from the cold. The cabin offered protection from the storm, but feed for the horses would soon be exhausted.

# A Blow Down



*And behold, the Lord passed by, and a great and strong wind tore into the mountains… but the Lord was not in the wind.* (I Kings 12:11)

They had been resting in the cabin for several days. Outside the sunshine had returned, but with it there was a warm wind that increased in intensity as the day progressed. Tyler had gone out just before noon to get more firewood. The pile on the leeward side of the house was getting smaller at an alarming rate, although they were not using as much wood now that the days and nights were warmer. Tyler thought again about the necessity of finding a warmer area to spend the winter. The horses would not be able to survive without grass to eat. They needed to leave as soon as the dirt roads were no longer muddy.

*Not yet*, thought Tyler, as he scrapped mud off his boot onto a rock. Just then a gust of wind caught him and nearly slammed him into the south wall of the cabin. Returning to the cabin quickly, Tyler dumped his load of logs into the firebox and put another log on the fire.

"Whew! It's really getting windy out there! Must be a Chinook wind because it feels warm. That means the wind is a "snow eater." Just what we need to finish melting the snow and dry up the ground. We need to move south quickly before winter sets in for good."

The howl of the wind was unmistakable. Tyler heard some commotion in the garage. The two horses and the pony were milling around nervously. He went over to pat each of them in an attempt to quiet them down. Wolf had begun to howl as if singing a duet with the wind. Tyler let him out of the garage. The last thing the horses needed was more noise.

Returning to tend the fireplace, he commented "I want everything in this cabin to be ship shape just like we found it." He concentrated on arranging the logs, then he cleaned the hearth and areas around the hearth. They had learned that this cabin belonged to the Wilsons. That explained why Little Red had been able to find it. She had been here before.

"Bam! Bam! Bam!" Several large thuds close to the cabin brought Tyler back to the subject of the wind.

Danny woke up from the nap he was taking in the loft. "Wow! What was that?"

Before Tyler could answer there were several more thuds. Now the thuds were almost continuous and seemed to surround the cabin.

The horses were clearly upset by the commotion outside. Both boys ran to the garage door just in time to see Mr. B rear and paw the air with his hooves. His hooves returned to ground but not before one of them grazed Little Red's flank. The pony squealed in pain and bared her teeth as she turned to bite the big black.

"Get her inside," Tyler ordered, as he tried to grab the black's halter.

Danny didn't wait. He grabbed Little Red's halter and coaxed her inside the cabin leaving Tyler to deal with the larger horses. Mr. B continued to lunge and rear, causing items to fall off the shelves. Some rolled under the hooves of both horses. Tyler knew he was in danger, but he refused to leave the horses as the commotion outside seemed to intensify.

Taking a peek outside the garage door, he saw trees being uprooted and falling all over the forest. The ground, still unfrozen in this fall storm, was saturated by the melted snow and gave no support when the wind caught the pines. Their shallow root system was no match for the force of the wind, and one after another they tumbled to the ground. In their fall some limbs collided with other trees helping to uproot them.

Tyler shut the door and turned his attention to the horses. Both were now rearing, bucking and milling around the garage spilling more stuff and becoming more agitated.

Finally, Tyler managed to grab Buck's halter. He tried to force him to bow and enter the low door of the house, but Buck had never been in the house, and he wasn't going in now. Tyler maintained a firm hold on the halter as he looked to see what Danny was doing with Little Red. He had climbed on the hassock and was stuffing a rolled washcloth in each of the pony's ears and praying softly "Help me, Jesus! Help me, Jesus!"

Amazingly, this strategy seemed to work. Little Red knelt down by the fireplace. She sat calmly and looked at the boys who were now both struggling with Buck.

"Great job, Danny! Get more washcloths." Danny ran to the bathroom and grabbed all that were there.

Tyler held Buck's head down, while Danny stood on the step that led to the house and stuffed a rolled cloth into each ear. In a few moments he began to quiet down, but Mr. B. was still raising a ruckus in the garage. Now Tyler slipped past Buck into the garage in attempt to quiet the largest horse.

He finally managed to get a washcloth in one ear. The horse tried desperately to dislodge it. By this time, the noise outside was beginning to diminish. The wind was finally dying down. Now there was only an occasional plop or thud.

Tyler turned his attention to the disaster on the garage floor. Some items had been ruined, pummeled by the hooves of the horses. He put these into a pile by the garage door. Other items had been punctured and had leaked all over the floor of the garage.

Tyler scooped up some of the black stuff on his finger and sniffed it! Oil! This had to be cleaned up or it would be a huge fire hazard. Cleaned up, yes, but how?

Poking around in a big bin at the back of the room, he found some rags that he used to soak up as much of the oil as he could. Now the problem was how to dispose of the rags. When the wind died down, he took the oil-soaked rags outside and poked them under one of the fallen trees. They were still a potential fire hazard, but not to the boys in the cabin, at least until the forest dried out more.

The boys spent the rest of the afternoon cleaning up the garage as well as they could and treating the nicks and scrapes on the horses. Most of them were small and would heal quickly. Fortunately, they had access to antiseptic from the bathroom in the cabin. Little Red's scrape was the worst. They washed it carefully and poured some antiseptic from the bathroom on one of the washcloths, and held it on the pony's flank. The horse flinched, but she had learned to trust Danny and submitted to this treatment.

# A Road Trip

September 26th

*Heal me, LORD, and I will be healed; save me and I will*
*be saved, for you are the one I praise.* (Jeremiah 17:14)

A dark blue sedan pulled up to the front entrance of Altitude Medical Center in Denver. The driver of the car sent a text message to the nursing station inside. Within a few minutes a nurse came out pushing a wheelchair. "I am so glad that you are able to find a place for her. The rehab/nursing homes in this area are very overcrowded. I guess that isn't the case in your part of the state?"

The driver, a man named Ted, answered, "No, we have had fewer Super Virus cases than you have and our hospitals, rehab centers and nursing homes are no more crowded than usual. We have made all the arrangements for her. It will take us between six and seven hours to drive there. Will she be ok?"

The nurse nodded. "She will probably want to sleep a lot. She has been through a lot, but she has been looking forward to this trip. She hasn't been out of the hospital in weeks."

The nurse closed the door on the passenger side, and the car slowly pulled away from the curb. The nurse stood waving for a few moments then turned and pushed the wheelchair back inside.

The passenger smiled weakly. "It is great just to be outside and to see the trees and the sky again. Thank you so much for making these arrangements for me. The 'Captain' will be back in a couple of weeks to take care of me. I can hardly wait!"

"We are looking forward to seeing him as well. Kyle and Kody are as eager to see him as we are. He is like a superhero to them."

"Have you heard anything about the boys?" she asked anxiously.

Ted silently shook his head as he turned onto I-70 going west.

The woman sighed and stared out the window as the car left the city and started into the foothills, and soon she was fast asleep.

After a brief stop at Silverthorne for burgers and coffee, their trip continued. The woman had little to say during the long trip. When her eyes were not closed, they were focused on the scene beyond the car window. She prayed silently for the towns and communities along the way.

The foothills quickly grew into tall pine and spruce-covered mountains that were sometimes capped with snow or shrouded with clouds. After the high passes had been traversed, the highway dropped into Glenwood Canyon and then into a terrain that was characterized by rolling hills and flat-top mesas partially covered by bushes and pinyon pine. The landscape continued to morph toward more desert-like terrain: beautiful sandstone cliffs carved in unusual formations with only an occasional dot of green in the predominately red landscape.

At last they pulled up to Pinyon Pine Rehab Center. After a call to the front desk, a nurse appeared with a wheelchair. The passenger slowly moved herself into the chair while her driver retrieved her personal belongings from the trunk. Before she was wheeled inside, Ted assured her that his family would come by for a visit as soon as she was settled in her room.

The woman smiled weakly and waved as she was wheeled into the home.

# The Switchbacks!

September 27th

> *I call on the Lord in my distress and He answers me.*
> (Psalm 120:1)

The need to find a warmer place away from the snow to spend the winter propelled them out after more than ten days in the cabin. Mr. B's scratch from the encounter with the cougar had responded well to Tyler's doctoring and the days of rest, and all the bandages had been removed from Wolf's ear. The scrapes all three horses had gotten in the garage were also responding well to treatment. They had been able to resupply some food, water, and other essentials, wash and dry their clothes, pack the summer items, and "borrow" some essential items from the Wilson's cabin.

Looking at the relief map on the wall that they had found in the cabin, they had located the quickest way off the plateau to lower, warmer ground. Now the horses seemed as eager as the boys to leave this wintery cold. Also, the knowledge that their nights would be spent out in the open without protection propelled them forward in search of lower altitude and warmer weather.

After about two hours, they came upon a very narrow road that led off the top of the plateau in a series of switch backs to the valley about two thousand feet below. This certainly would be the fastest way down. However, it was clear that the horses were reluctant to go down this way. Tyler was able to urge Buck onto the narrow road and down the first switchback. Little Red with Danny in the saddle came next with Wolf and Mr. B bringing up the rear. The road narrowed as they continued down. At the same time the drop off steepened and became more frightening.

Danny complained, "My right foot is hanging out over empty space, and it is a long way down. I'm scared! Don>t slip Little Red. Be careful, Little Red. I do NOT want to fall into another canyon."

The whole group had passed the third switchback and were well down on the third leg of the road, when Tyler cried out, "Stop! The road is washed out!"

Most of the road was gone along a four-foot stretch, and only a very narrow strip remained close to the cliff face. Tyler dismounted and Buck took the challenge, backed up, ran, and leaped over the gap. His front hooves landed on firm ground, but his back hooves caused more of the road to collapse as he pulled himself up the rest of the way over the gap. Tyler came next walking carefully along the remaining narrow strip of road next to the cliff face. Wolf ran along the narrow ledge and soon bypassed the washout.

Next it was Little Red's turn. Danny dismounted, and he inched along as Tyler had, hugging the cliff. Little Red carefully followed behind Danny. Only Mr. B. remained. His greater weight was causing even the ground beneath his hooves to slump, fail, and slide down the steep embankment. He was too heavy to jump the growing gap in the road, and he was too big to turn around on the narrow road. His fear showed in his wide eyes, and he snorted and pawed the air with one of his enormous hooves.

Seeing the fear in the eyes of Mr. B, Danny breathed a quick prayer: "Help Mr. B, God." It was Wolf who saved the day. He ran back over the narrow strip of ground next to the cliff and began to jump and bark at Mr. B who took a couple of steps backwards. Wolf barked again, and Mr. B backed up again. Then Mr. B seemed to get it. He remembered his days as a show horse in the arena, prancing backwards in response to his trainer's commands. Now he pranced backwards up the narrow incline with all the confidence of the show horse he had once been with Wolf barking triumphantly at his front hooves.

Mr. B snorted when he reached the first switchback and trotted forward easily making the larger turns up the remaining two legs of the journey to regain the top of the mesa. Tyler and Danny lost sight of the enormous horse and the wolf dog after that. The group had been forced to split for the first time in their journey from Denver.

Tyler and Danny continued on down the narrow switchbacks and reached the bottom safely. Already the air temperature seemed warmer, and the wind less penetrating. The road continued gradually downhill for a few miles. It was easy going and the two horses and their riders made good time. They often paused and looked back to see if they could spot Mr. B and Wolf.

Tyler was eager to make camp a little early. It would give Mr. B and Wolf a chance to catch up. It was only then that they discovered that their camping gear was still on Mr. B! They had limited food, and plenty of water, but no sleeping bags or tent. They took the saddles off the horses and used them for pillows while covering themselves with the saddle blankets. The ground was rocky and had an occasional prickly cactus that made the sleeping spot more undesirable.

Danny began complaining as usual, then he stopped. Maybe God could still save the horse and dog. He started to pray loudly in his high-pitched voice, "God, please help Mr. B and Wolf. We love them and need them, and they need us too. (His voice was escalating in volume and intensity.) We are sorry we made Mr. B go down the narrow road. We promise to…"

Tyler interrupted, "Shh! Shh!

Danny retorted, "You never want me to pray. You always…"

Tyler interrupted again. "Be quiet and listen."

"What?"

Little Red and Buck had both stopped grazing. Their heads were raised, and they were looking in the same direction. Their ears were turned to catch the sound.

Then they all heard it, very quiet at first, then louder and louder, now unmistakable, "Woof, woof!"

Danny fairly shouted! "It's Wolf, it's Wolf! They found us! They found us! They found us!" Danny danced—a silhouetted figure in the light of the beautiful red and golden sunset.

Now in the fading light, they could just make out the shapes of the large, black horse with the wolf dog running and jumping at his side! A second dog-shaped animal followed close behind. They were coming in fast now, the animals running at top speed.

Within minutes Tyler was hugging Mr. B's muzzle. The horse snorted loudly and shook his head. He was lathered with sweat and foaming lightly at the mouth. He received the water poured into the pan gladly: just a sip for now. More would come later when he had cooled down.

Wolf was jumping and barking. No one had ever seen him so excited. He ran from Tyler to Danny jumping up on them and trying to lick their faces. Then he ran from Buck to Little Red barking and jumping. Little Red started running around in circles, while Tyler walked Mr. B to cool him down. Lady had disappeared again into the growing shadows of evening.

Tyler laughed as he affectionately patted the huge, black horse, "It's about time you got here with our tent and sleeping bags!"

The significance of the situation dawned on Danny. "They came when I prayed. God heard me when I prayed!"

Tyler laughed and put his arm around Danny, "More likely, Wolf heard you when you shouted!" He gave Danny a friendly "nuggie" on his head.

Danny laughed and snuggled into Tyler, the tension between them melting, "Yes, but God made Wolf hear me when I shouted!"

Still laughing, Tyler relaxed and relented his position on divine intervention. "You know, little buddy, this time I think you just might be right!"

# Forest Fire!

September 28th morning

*When you walk through the fire, you will not be burned,*
*the flames will not set you ablaze.* (Isaiah 43:2)

Their journey had taken them south and west into the canyonlands along the Delores River. Morning came, crisp and bright. Danny was the first to notice the fresh snow on the mountain tops. Though beautiful, this only heightened Tyler's concern for the weather that lay ahead. They had been through one snowstorm, and one was more than enough. Even at this lower altitude the days were getting cooler, and the nights were downright cold. "We can't last through the winter here. We won't make it through the next snowstorm. Finally, Tyler exclaimed, "I just don't know what to do!"

"Look! Over there! Smoke," Danny shouted.

Tyler looked where Danny was pointing. An innocent-looking white plume was winding its way up through the junipers and bushes.

"Must be a campfire," Tyler commented.

They watched transfixed for about fifteen minutes as the smoke plume grew, and flame appeared beneath it. The fire was beginning to spread up the hillside. The wind was fanning sparks ahead of the fire-- sparks that ignited dried wood on the mesa flank, dry leaves, and even the tops of the few trees present in the landscape.

A gust of wind carried a spark across to the hillside where Tyler and Danny had been grazing their horses. Within minutes, the fire had spread to their side of the valley.

Mr. B gave a big snort and started off down the slope. The other horses had become noticeably nervous and were stamping and snorting as Danny and Tyler mounted. Soon all three steeds were galloping toward the base of the hill.

"Where are we going?" Danny called as he struggled to maintain his feet in the stirrups and his balance on Little Red.

"Don't know. Guess we will find out!"

The horses had reached a little ridge above a small river. The drop to the river at this point was about twenty feet down a steep slope of loose gravel. As boys and horses seemed to be judging what to do next, the fire broke over the ridge behind them, and a shift in the wind sent a big plume of smoke in their direction.

Again, Mr. B gave a snort. He jumped on to the slope all four legs held stiff. Another jump took him about one-third of the remaining way to the river. Before he could reach the river, the other two horses jumped onto the slope of loose gravel, and, using Mr. B's technique, were also on their way to the river.

Wolf could be heard barking furiously a distance up the ridge, perhaps warning the animals to get out. Soon he and several deer, two antelope, a badger, and two foxes and a wolf plunged into the river with the horses.

The group continued upstream walking in the safety of the small river. As they rounded a bend, they heard a roar of rapidly moving water. Continuing upstream the noise increased drowning the crackling of the fire on the riverbanks above them.

It was Danny who first spotted the falls. There, directly ahead of them, just visible through the tall trees lining the river bank was a 30-foot falls, and they were headed right for the plunge pool at the base of it.

Meanwhile, the fire was increasing in intensity in the surrounding forests. Arriving at the plunge pool, the little group admired the beauty of the falls and felt the welcome spray of water droplets covering every part of their bodies. They had found the ideal protection from the fire. The group continued to admire the beauty of the falls as the forest around them burned.

Tyler commented, "One thing I will have to say is even though I miss my video games, they could never compare with the real-life adventures we have had. I love these horses and Wolf. I am even learning to put up with you, Danny! Tyler chuckled. What a summer this has been!"

Danny was quick to agree. "The only thing missing is my mommy!"

Once the fire had died out on the river banks on either side of the pool, they started downstream once again being careful to stay in the middle of the river and avoid the still smoldering riverbanks.

Mr. B continued to forge ahead as though he was an old hand in dealing with forest fires. He pushed ahead as quickly as conditions would allow. After about half an hour of trudging along the stream bed, they found themselves on the valley floor. From here the river began a series of meanders as it traversed the flat land.

# Narrow Escape



September 28th afternoon

*Lord, how many are my foes! How many rise up against me!* (Psalm 3:1)

Wishing to push ahead quickly and leave the fire far behind, they left the riverbed in favor of a small dirt road. It wasn't long after they had allowed themselves to be out in the open that the sound of a chopper was heard. Was the chopper looking for them or for anyone disobeying the quarantine? Once again, a choice had to be made. Would they continue out in the open or duck back into whatever protection the juniper and pinyon trees offered?

Little Red bolted ahead to a series of cliffs on the left side of the valley. There some jutting rocks provided at least a measure of protection. They reached the cliffs, Tyler pulled off the saddles, freed the horses and ducked down trying to blend into the rock formation.

Meanwhile the horses galloped to a nearby meadow. Mr. B rolled on his back scratching where his skin itched. Little Red loped away from the other horses as if she knew she should not be to part of a recognizable group.

The chopper made several rounds, then left the area by way of the valley ahead.

When the chopper was gone, the horses returned to the rocks. Tyler had spread out their wet gear to dry. "We can't use this stuff until it gets dry," he said, rubbing the saddles down with saddle soap. We will camp here tonight.

Danny gave an anxious look at the burning hills behind them. "Do we have enough time? That was awful back there!"

The wind died down as dusk approached, and the fire laid down. The two made camp confident that their horses would wake them if there was a problem.

After they had eaten a roasted rabbit, they felt confident enough to allow themselves a good night's sleep.

# Going Shopping



*And my God will meet all your needs according to the
riches of his glory in Christ Jesus.* (Philippians 4:19*)*

Upon awakening, Tyler called to Danny, "Get up now. The fire is
advancing again, and I don't see the horses."

That last statement caused Danny to sit up and begin to look
for his precious Little Red. "There they are down by the river!"

"Something is wrong. The horses aren't coming back!" Tyler looked
around. There just below them in the rocks was a cougar crouched ready
to spring. He had his eye on the horses, but occasionally looked in the
direction of the boys.

Tyler picked up several rocks and began throwing them at the
cougar. Danny quickly followed suit. The cougar turned and ran. The
boys were not certain that it had left the area.

Once back in the saddle, they gave their full attention to the fire. It
was moving toward them again. They were not safe yet.

The group rode toward a small town. They had tried to avoid
contact with people on this trip, but it looked like the fire was headed
right toward this town, and there might be no one outside the town to
spot the fire and warn them. Cell phone and land line coverage seemed
to be spotty.

Tyler decided to change to his school pull-over sweater so that he
would not look like a bum that had been riding in the back country

for weeks. He took the time to shave his peach fuzz and trim his hair. He would use this opportunity to load up on essential supplies as well. Checking their cash, he saw that they had only enough to buy another week's supply of groceries.

He found a small store on the outskirts of town, purchased more bars, jerky, apples and carrots. As he was checking out, he pointed out the window to the growing plume of smoke. "Any idea what that is?"

The grocer looked. "Huh! No!" He ran out of the store and into the next store, a small hardware store. Both store owners came out and shook their heads. "How long has that been there," they asked?

Tyler shrugged, "Just noticed it as I walked in." Something told him not to give too much information. Leaving the store with his purchased items, he walked down the road. Then when he was out of sight, he headed into the trees and doubled back to rejoin his brother and their animals.

On a pinnacle overlooking the town, they saw a fire truck that someone had managed to fill with gas, along with several men on horseback go into the fire area.

"Is that all the equipment they have? They stand no chance with that."

The group headed on down the valley away from the fire and toward a second small town. Tyler again went into a small store. This time the grocer questioned him closely. "Heard that some kids up in the hills started the fire. You didn't see anybody on your way here, did you?"

"No," Tyler said. "I came up from the south. You should see the fire from a few miles down the road. Looks like the whole mountain is on fire."

Again, Tyler doubled back to join the group. "At the rate it is growing, the fire will reach this area sometime tomorrow or the next day. The folks down there are looking for some kids that they say started it. We better lay low until this all blows over."

It was still light when Tyler decided to call it a day. They pulled off the road. It had been windy, and the temperature had been dropping especially in the afternoon. Even here, at this lower altitude, fall was certainly in the air. They were going to need a good shelter for the cold night that they were certain was coming. Tyler located a large boulder and popped open the tent on the leeward side of it. The wind, even in this protected spot, was whipping the sides of the tent. They would never be able to sleep with all that racket. They would need more shelter.

Tyler looked at the long slender trunks of the lodge pole pines near the rock. He picked up a broken pole from the ground and laced it between two of the standing trees. Then Danny got the idea, and he began poking branches between the pole and the ground while Tyler found more poles and laced them between the standing pines. After an hour's work, they crawled inside their make-shift lean-to. It was amazing how much of the wind was blocked by their simple efforts with the pine branches. This would be a much more protected place to spend the blustery night.

The horses, unbothered by the wind, were happy to roll on their backs once their saddles had been removed and began grazing.

# Dust Devil

September 30th

*You will seek me and find me when you seek me with all your heart.* (Jeremiah, 29:13)

Morning brought a new thought to Tyler as he saddled the horses. *I wonder if the quarantine has been lifted. There certainly was no issue in the town I visited yesterday.* As if in answer to his question, he heard sirens: not just one but several. Looking down the slope, he saw several fire trucks on the highway making their way up to the fire. Several trucks and cars with volunteers followed them. The quarantine had been lifted, at least here in this place!

The morning was warm, and the wind was calm. The group was making good progress and by mid- afternoon had accomplished their distance goal for the day. Danny was the first to notice a brown cloud approaching from the west. It was so different from the storm clouds they had seen, that he remarked immediately to Tyler that something new was coming. The animals were all aware by this time. They seemed determined to outrun it and started off at a full gallop in the opposite direction.

Just as the dust-filled wind swirled about them, Danny cried out, "God, help!" He spied an old shack just off the road. It pitched at a strange angle, but it's door still squeaked open admitting all of them. They squeezed inside and managed to push the door shut. The shack had multiple cracks between the boards and through these they could see that the sky had darkening outside.

Now the full force of the storm was upon them. Even inside the shack, Tyler and Danny had to pull their shirts over their mouths and noses. They sat on the floor, their hands over their heads, protecting their faces. The animals protected their noses by all facing inward, their brushing tails closest to the walls of the building. Within minutes it was over, and the dust began to settle.

A little later, Tyler cautiously opened the door to reveal a cloudless blue sky and no wind. The dust was swirling down, covering everything with a layer of brown. The "dust devil" was making its way to the south pushed by the prevailing winds. Once again, they had escaped harm.

Dusk was approaching when the boys pulled their horses over and dismounted. Tyler had spotted a grove of trees near the river. They set up camp quickly since both boys were tired. Soon they were in their tent munching on dried jerky. Danny fell asleep, but Tyler's mind was working overtime. The storm today had increased his concern about the coming fall and winter months. They had managed to escape many dangers, but would their luck hold? Or was it, as Danny kept insisting, really all the result of answered prayer.

Tyler thought about the likelihood of so many escapes from danger on one trip. Maybe it was not God, but what if it was? He had prayed at Black Canyon and had seen Danny pulled up from what might have been a plunge to his death. He felt an urging to pray again. This time it would not be to save his brother but to save himself. "God, I know you sent your Son Jesus to die for me. He got the punishment that I deserved. I ask for forgiveness for the wrong things I have done and for doubting You. I ask Jesus to come into my heart and life. Thank you, Jesus, for coming in."

Immediately peace flooded Tyler's heart and mind. "Oh, and just one more request: Help us find a home! Thank you for all the help so far." Tyler's mind quit racing. Their future was in God's hands.

# Where are They?



"Ask and it will be given to you; seek and you will find;" (Matthew 7:7)

Kyle (age 12) and Kody (age 10) met their dad at the door as he returned from work. "Did you see her today? Is she getting better?"

Ted, the boys' dad, answered cautiously, "It will take her time to get used to her new surroundings at the rehab center. After all she has only been at the center for a few days."

"How about our uncle, the Captain? When does he get back from the army? I can't wait to see him. He is like Captain Marvel or Super Man." Kyle's voice was full of enthusiasm.

"Yes, he is our superhero," Kody exclaimed.

Ted took off his jacket. The weather was getting cooler now that September was nearly over. "I think my brother should be home in a week or so. I am as eager to see him as you are."

"What about our cousins? We have one cousin whom we haven't seen in three years and another cousin that we have never met. When are we going to see our cousins? Are they coming with Uncle Cap? Are they still lost in the mountains? Now that our neighbors left on a camping trip, we need someone to play with."

Ted sat down in his favorite chair and let out a sigh. "I only wish that I could promise when those cousins of yours are going to show up.

It had better be soon, because winter is coming. At least we will have your aunt and uncle close by. The Captain is going to buy a ranch west of town."

The boys jumped up and down with enthusiasm. "Now we just need our cousins."

Ted switched on the evening news. They had been listening carefully for some news of the cousins, but so far there had been nothing concrete. There had been possible sightings at South Park and at Black Canyon of the Gunnison, but no one had verified the sightings.

The news did verify that the threat of the Super Virus was currently very low in their area. Many people were availing themselves of the vaccine that was now available at most clinics and doctors' offices.

When Barb, the boys' mother, called for dinner the boys continued their questions. "Does the Captain's oldest boy look like him? Does he look like us? I can't remember."

"And how about the cousin we have never met? Does he have blond hair or brown?

Ted smiled at their enthusiasm. "I think the Captain's oldest boy has dark blond hair, like the rest of our family. The other boy has dark brown hair, I believe."

"Will they like Legos? Will they like to ride bikes? Will they play Hide and Seek with us?"

Ted turned more sober, afraid that his boys would be disappointed. "I think that Captain's oldest boy likes video games. I have heard that He is a loner. And the younger one? Hmm. I have heard that he is a real talker. You can't shut him up. Those boys have been riding all summer. They may have changed." He added hopefully.

"Let's pray for our cousins. Let's pray for the Captain and all his family. God can make all this turn out good, right?"

# A Camper



> *Whoever welcomes a little child like this in My name,*
> *welcomes Me.* (Matthew 18:5)

Tyler and Danny maneuvered their mounts around a red rock formation and along the stream where the brush was the heaviest. They needed the brush to give them good cover. Wolf suddenly took off from the group and climbed one of the rock mounds nearby. From that vantage point he could see something that Tyler and Danny were not able to see, and began barking. Tyler dismounted and scrambled up the rock to see what was bothering the dog. He seldom barked because he was aware, as they all were, that they needed to attract as little attention as possible.

"Well, look at this!" Tyler exclaimed at Danny crawled up beside him.

There in the valley on the opposite side of the rock was a small travel trailer pulled by a truck. Even from a distance it was clear that a family had been camping there but had not kept their campsite very clean.

As Danny and Tyler cautiously approached the campsite, they saw that the area had probably been attacked by coyotes that had pulled food from the camper making the site a mess.

A few yards closer, several coyotes came out of hiding and stealthily approach the boys. Tyler and Danny were ready. Each picked up a small rock and threw them at the coyotes. Their hours of practice paid off as the rocks hit their targets. The boys kept throwing rocks until there were no more coyotes. Tyler was glad that they had not fired their gun that would certainly have attracted attention. They slipped off their mounts and continued their approach on foot. An unmistakable stench greeted their nostrils. Something or someone had died here!

Suddenly a small girl around three-years-old and covered in grease and blood emerged from under the vehicle. She approached them calling "Help me! Help me"

"Where is your mommy?" Tyler asked.

The girl pointed to some bones interspersed with pieces of torn clothing lying on the ground a short distance from the trailer. "There, but she broke! She not get up. There's Stevie, and Jessie. They all broke and smell bad!"

Some dried blood remained but most of it had been licked up by the coyotes who had been feeding on the carcasses.

Tyler turned away. "Let's get out of here!'

The girl began to wail, "No, don't leave, don't leave. Who take care of me?"

At that moment Wolf ran up to the girl and began to lick her face. At first the boys thought that the large dog was planning to eat the little girl, but he was only cleaning her face. He continued licking, cleaning the front of her overalls.

"Wait," Danny shouted! "We can't leave her. She will die."

"I'm not going anywhere near that stinky thing," Tyler declared firmly.

"What if I clean her up?" Danny asked hopefully.

"I have clothes," the girl declared. She climbed up the steps of the trailer and disappeared inside.

In a few minutes, she appeared again at the door with some clean, bright-colored play clothes.

"That's it!" Danny exclaimed. "I will take her to one of those potholes in the red rock formation that we just passed. They are filled with rainwater that should be warm from the afternoon sun. I can wash her there."

He took the little girl's hand and helped her scramble up the rock to the potholes. He helped her remove her outer garments, then submerged her body in the first pothole.

Tyler threw Danny a bar of soap all the while maintaining his distance. He was remembering his commitment to Jesus of the night before. Jesus loved him. Did Jesus want him to show love to this strange little girl?

Danny soaked and washed the girl's stringy blond hair, her face, arms and legs. Then he gently lifted her out and put her in another pothole nearby. This water provided the rinse that she needed. Danny then lifted her out of the second pothole and left her sitting on the rock to dry.

He rummaged around in their packs until he found some string which he took back to the rock. He brushed the girl's hair removing the tangles, parted it down the middle and pulled half of the hair to one side where he tied it with the string. Then he went to work on the other side giving the girl two ponytails.

Next Danny helped her put on a cute pink t-shirt and shorts to match. "There! Is she clean enough for you?"

Tyler could not believe the transformation. Wolf barked encouragingly. Tyler was outnumbered. Jesus, Danny and Wolf voted in favor of the girl.

"I, Emma," the girl declared confidently. "You like Emma, now?"

"How long have you been here?" Tyler asked. The girl shook her head. "We thought we safe. Then bad guys come. They want gas. They shoot guns. Mommy say, "Hide under truck. I climb inside." She pointed to the engine block.

"Bad guys not see Emma. When bad guys gone, I eat crackers and cookies. I drink pop. See!" She opened the refrigerator to show the rotting food. Clearly, she had been on her own for a few days.

"See, I got food." She opened a cupboard in the trailer to reveal a few cans of spaghetti, soup, and boxes of cold cereal. "You want?"

Even Tyler was willing to brave the odor to claim the food. Their supplies were getting very low. This would provide for a few more days.

After they had loaded the food into Mr. B's pack, they retrieved Emma's car seat from the pickup and tied it on Buck behind Tyler's saddle. Tyler started to lift the girl onto the horse.

"No, wait! I need kitty."

Emma struggled free of Tyler's grasp and ran to a cushion inside the truck.

"No, this one no good!" She said throwing out an obviously dead kitten. "This one no good!" She continued to sort through the pile of dead kittens next to their dying mother. "Here's one!" she exclaimed. She held up a pitiful kitten, dirty, and nearly dead.

"Ugh!" Tyler exclaimed. "Let's get out of here."

Once again Wolf intervened. He took the pitiful kitten in his mouth. Carefully, he carried the tiny bundle to a near-by rock where he had been chewing on what remained of his last catch, a jack rabbit.

"No," Emma cried! "Don't eat Kitty!"

Before anyone could stop Wolf, he took another bite of the rabbit, chewed it for a while, then spat it out in front of the kitten. With his paw, he gently pushed the kitten's head into the regurgitated food. At first the kitten seemed not to understand. At last, her little pink tongue came out and she began to lap at the food, cautiously at first, then eagerly.

When she had finished eating, Wolf began to lick the tiny animal. Soon the kitten was a cute, gray, fuzzy ball, purring softly.

When the group got underway, Wolf carried the kitten by the nap of her neck in his mouth as though he had just received a prize to protect. Would he show the kitten to his mysterious Lady?

# Emma and Kitty

October 2nd

*A little child shall lead them.* (Isaiah 11:6)

*See to it that you do not look down on these little ones.*
*For I tell you that their angels in Heaven always see the*
*face of my Father in Heaven.* (Matthew 18:10)

They had gone a few miles in silence. Emma soon fell asleep in her rear-facing position. Suddenly she awoke, pointed with her little finger, and exclaimed in a loud whisper, "bad guys!"

Danny, who was riding behind Tyler, turned around to look where she was pointing. A black sedan was coming over the rise behind them approaching slowly. "We have company. We have to get out of here."

"Quick, into that wind cave up there." With a silent prayer, Tyler pulled Buck off the trail and toward the cave. The rest of the group scrambled up to the cave and pushed back into the shadows.

Unfortunately, though the ceiling was high, the wind cave was not very deep. The shadows at the back barely covered the little group.

The sedan followed the road that took them to a parking area above the cave. A couple of the men got out of the car and walked to the edge of the mesa. "I thought I saw something down there," commented one of the men.

Suddenly there was a low growl followed by a hiss. One of the men above exclaimed, "A cat! Come on, let's get out of here."

Tyler and Danny looked with amazement at Kitty.

"Did she do that?" Tyler whispered?

Another low growl.

"Yep, that's her all right!" Tyler's whisper was louder, bolder. "Welcome to the team, Emma and Kitty! You guys rock!" Who would have guessed that God could use such unlikely characters as Emma and Kitty to protect them? Danny and Tyler were about to find out that God planned to use Emma in even more unusual ways.

# Cousins!



October 4th

> *Do not forsake your friend or a friend of your family,*
> (Proverbs 27:10)

Several nights later they were enjoying some roasted rabbit legs while sitting around their little fire. The weather was mild. The hills were lower and rolling in this part of the state. Lots of pinyon pine and juniper and even some prickly pear and other cactus provided cover for the hills.

Emma came up and sat next to Tyler. She studied one side of his face carefully, then looked at the other side. Tyler was beginning to feel a little self-conscious. "What's wrong?' he asked."

"You know Kyle?" Emma asked.

"Kyle, Kyle who," Tyler replied.

"Kyle has green house and brother Kody. You look like Kyle."

Tyler looked surprised. "I don't think I know any Kyle, or Kody or green…what a minute. I did visit a cousin named Kyle. Yes, he did have a brother named Kody…And yes I am sure he lived in a green house."

"Emma play with Kyle and Kody. Then mommy say 'time to leave.' We go camping, then bad guys come…then mommy got broke, daddy got broke. Emma cry."

Tyler was intrigued. This little girl had recently played with his cousins, the children of his father's brother, Ted! "Wasn't their last name "Cummins," or "Carter," or "Cartright," or…? I can't remember. Still

I think we need to try to find them. Maybe they can give us shelter, especially now that the quarantine seems to be lifted."

He couldn't remember where his cousins lived. They had not visited these cousins since his mother's death three years earlier. Venturing across a paved highway, they noticed the sign that claimed that Cortez was sixty-miles to the south. Was that it? Did his cousins live in Cortez? That name was clearly familiar. Wow! Now they had a destination: one that was reachable in about three days of hard riding.

Still cautious about being seen and picked up, they kept off the road and tried to stay hidden in the trees. The vegetation was sparse here in southwestern Colorado, but the flanks of the rivers were lined with cottonwoods. The gloriously colored leaves were falling off even in this southern part of the state and at this lower altitude.

Danny and Little Red continued to be drawn to every pile of leaves insisting on tromping through them.

The weather for once seemed to be cooperating. A balmy breeze blew, and the sky was partially filled with fluffy cumulus clouds. Tyler hoped that they would have the time they needed to reach his cousins house before another major storm set in. Their food reserves were also getting low again in spite of the reinforcements from Emma's camper. He remembered his prayer. He could depend on God, couldn't he? This area sometimes got snow, but the chances were not nearly as great as at higher altitudes from which they had just come.

# Gramps!

October 8th



*He and all his family were devout and God-fearing.*
(Acts 10:2)

They approached a river to give the horses a drink. Seated on the riverbank fishing was an older gentleman and a boy. The boy, who appeared to be about Danny's age, was talking non-stop to the older man.

"Do you think they will ever find them? What did Aunt Marianne say about their appearance? Does Tyler really have blond hair like me? I think Danny has brown hair. I have never seen him, and he is my own cousin." The questions continued to flow. "Where were they last seen? Are they criminals? Will they be put in jail?"

Immediately Emma began to squirm in her car seat. "Emma want down. Now!" Thinking that she needed to go to the bathroom, Tyler released her from her seat and carefully set her on the ground. Immediately she ran up to the older man and threw her tiny arms around him, "Gramps!"

Surprised, the older man, held her at arm's length then pulled her to himself!! "Emma! How can this be you? We thought your family was all dead. The report was that vandals had invaded your family camp site and killed everyone in order to steal your gasoline."

Emma stood confident and as tall as her short stature would permit. "Bad men come. Shot guns! Mommy got broke. Daddy got broke. Stevie and Jessie got broke. Emma hide. Emma not get broke!!!! See!" She held out her hands.

Meanwhile, Kody ran up to Tyler. "Thank you for saving Emma! She was my neighbor." Then he stepped back. "Wait, don't I know you from somewhere. You look so familiar." The boy looked carefully at Tyler.

"Tyler? Your dad is Chris Cunningham, right? Is it really you, cousin? And you are still alive! Here you are standing in front of me! It's a miracle of God! Your Dad has had us looking everywhere for you."

Kody put one arm around Tyler and one around Danny. "Who is this?" he asked about Danny.

"Danny is my…"

Danny spoke up. "I am Tyler's stepbrother. After Tyler's mom died, his dad married my mom, Marianne."

Tyler interrupted with a smile. "Nope, he is my brother. No one ever had a better brother than Danny here. He helped me through lots of adventures the last few months, and he helped me find my heavenly Father, God!"

"My Dad will be so glad that you guys have been found safe and sound. He has been looking hard because you are his brother's children!" Kody gave both boys a hug.

The older gentlemen wasted no time calling on his cell phone. "I think we have found them." Yes, we are here at Cottonwood Park fishing on the Delores River."

He was still on the phone when he grabbed Kody and pulled him away from Tyler. "Don't touch him! They may be carrying the virus. Emma is probably too young to be infected."

A few minutes later, a patrol car turned into the parking area, and two cops emerged from the car. One of them approached the boys. "You need to come with us. We have been searching everywhere for you. Choppers, squad cars, mounted deputies. You name it. We have sent it."

"Are we in trouble?" Danny asked. "We didn't mean to do anything. We are going to return the Wilson's horses and their dog. But we still need them until we can find a place to live."

The cop took hold of Tyler's shoulder and pushed him into the car. The boys could not tell if they were in trouble but each of them was offering up a silent prayer.

"What about our horses," Danny cried.

"We are sending a trailer for them," the patrolman replied.

# Getting Checked Out

October 9th morning

*Then you will know the truth and the truth will set you free.* (John 8:32)

They rode in silence in the car and were ushered into the station in Cortez. "We need to make a positive identification, then we need to scoot these two off to the hospital to be tested," the driver of the car said.

The woman at the desk, maintaining social distance, began to look through the boys' school photos from their files. It didn't take long to make positive identifications. Then the boys were taken into separate interrogation rooms where they were questioned remotely to avoid the spread of any disease they may have contracted on their journey.

The boys answered questions about their trip and the incidents on the trip. The first thing they were asked is about the fire on the west side of Uncompahgre Plateau. Danny, of course, did not know any of the locations or geography, but his description of the smoke column that was the first evidence of the fire and all they had done to avoid being trapped by the fire convinced the officials that the boys had not set the fire. Why would they when the fire might bring possible harm to themselves?

Tyler, on the other hand, was very tight lipped about the whole journey from Denver, often answering with only one word, giving the supposed path of their travels. Both sessions were recorded, and later compared. Danny's account helped immensely to fill in the details of their trip.

Next the boys were sped off to the hospital in Cortez where they were quarantined in separate rooms and a series of tests were run on each of them.

The result was that Tyler tested positive for having contacted the Super Virus. However, he had obviously recovered from a very light case. Danny tested negative, but since he had been with Tyler for the last four months, it was assumed that he had a natural immunity. Both boys possessed antibodies that insured they would never catch the disease.

Tyler remembered being sick and having vomited but had attributed the whole incident to having eaten poorly-cooked rabbit.

# Reunion!



*How good and pleasant it is when brothers live together
in unity!* (Psalm 133:1)

*God sets the lonely in families.* (Psalm 68:6)

The hospital technician released each boy from his room and led them into the lobby. "We have someone here who wants to see you," he said.

The boys walked apprehensively into the lobby. Tyler heard a very familiar voice, "Tyler!" He turned quickly to see a large man standing in his full military uniform: Tyler's dad! He was holding out his arms to both boys. They both ran to him and snuggled up against him. Tears of relief streamed down Tyler's face. He had been anxious for weeks about how they would survive the winter. He had been breathing silent prayers to Jesus.

"Answers to your prayers, Danny!" he whispered softly giving his brother a hug.

"And that is not all," commented Captain Cunningham. "Here is someone you thought you would never see again." A nurse entered the room pushing a woman in a wheelchair.

At first both boys seemed puzzled. Who was this gaunt, but broadly smiling woman? Then she spoke, "Danny, Tyler!" It was Marianne, Danny's mother!

Both boys ran to her, and the tears grew more intense. It seemed too good to be true.

"I am so sorry," she whispered weakly. "I was unconscious, in a coma for weeks. A technician even thought that I had died. It was only recently that I regained consciousness and began to have the authorities look for you. I prayed for your safety, and now look! Jesus has answered my prayers! I have been living in Pinyon Pine Rehab Center since Ned, Cap's brother, drove me here from Denver. Soon I will be out of the center and out of this wheelchair! Jesus is restoring my health."

"He is answering your prayers and ours too," Tyler smiled with a quick glance at his father. The look of love and gratitude in his father's eyes was all the assurance he needed to know that his dad had also become a believer, one who had his prayers answered."

The reunion was taking center stage, but over at the side of the room Gramps stood with his arm around Emma. She had a firm hold on Kitty. Next to them stood Kyle and Kody so excited that they could barely stand still.

"I am buying a ranch house on a piece of ground in western Cortez. We can go on lots of nice fishing trips from there," Captain Cunningham offered.

"Will there be room for the horses?" Danny asked. "Little Red has been taking care of me, and now I want to take care of her."

"I thought those horses belonged to the Wilsons. They will probably return for them or have them sold. We have contacted them."

Danny went over to a chair and began to weep with his head in his hands.

The police captain walked into the room. "Looks like we have gotten a quick answer from the Wilsons. They texted us that they are not coming back to the States. They are selling their ranch and are glad that you have taken care of their horses. They want to give them to you, if you can accommodate them."

Chris Cunningham smiled. "I loved riding horseback when I was a kid. I wonder if that big black will do well under a saddle?"

Tyler ran to his dad. "Oh, Dad! We will have such fun. You will love Mr. B. A big man for a big horse!!"

Now Gramps came forward with Emma. "Emma wants to say goodbye."

"No, I don't," Emma cried. "I want stay with boys. I want stay with horses. Kitty wants stay with doggie. I want stay."

Marianne maneuvered her wheelchair in front of the child. "Hi, I am Marianne. Do I know you?"

Emma threw her arms around the woman. "Can I call you, mama? Please?"

Marianne smiled broadly. "I never had a little girl, but I always wanted one with blond hair just like you. Let's see what my boys say. Well, boys…"

She didn't have to finish. First Danny and then Tyler rushed to hug Emma.

"You have to come with us, Emma! Please, Dad, can she come? Please."

The large captain stooped down and swept the little child into his arms. "Of course, she can come. Marianne needs a little support on the female side of the ledger. She will need help with the dishes and the cooking. Right, Marianne?"

"Oh, Chris, really can we adopt her?" Marianne cried.

The security official stepped forward: "Emma's family was murdered, and she has no next of kin. All she has are Gramps here and Kyle and Kody's family who were her neighbors. I guess it will be up to them."

Kyle and Kody rushed forward eager to at last be a part of the conversation. "She was our neighbor, and now she wants to be our cousin. Oh, can she, can she?"

The police captain remarked, "Looks like all are in favor, so that would be a 'yes.' We will have the forms prepared for you, Mr. and Mrs. Cunningham."

"Thank you, Jesus," the whole group simultaneously muttered.

"It's going to be wonderful Thanksgiving this year," Gramps remarked. "Wait until we get all the cousins together."

"Out at my ranch, riding the horses with Wolf catching frisbees instead of rabbits." Captain Cunningham exclaimed.

"Our family grew over night," Tyler remarked.

"And don't forget God, Our Father in Heaven," Danny replied.

"We can't forget Him!" Tyler remarked. "He is the One who made all this happen." Tyler bowed his head. "Thank you, Father, God, for giving me the best family ever!!"

"Amen!" All in the room agreed.

The Wilson's Little Cabin